Secrets Revealed

By

Sarah Jane Gross

Author's Note:

While this book is largely fictitious,
I do pay tribute to family members
long gone, who we loved and cherished.

Dedication

In honor of Nora Benn Lewelling,
who lost one family but gained another through
marriage to a loving husband and motherhood.

Table of Contents

The rain on the tree boughs,
The whistle in the wind;
The flowers on the sill,
The dew on the glass rim.
Where do our secrets go?
In ordinary things.

-May Bell Sebastian, 1896 (Collection of Poems)

Chapter 1

Marshfield, Oregon

Coos County, Oregon, February 1921

The rain was coming down steadily along the southern coast of Oregon. Marshfield, a quaint and picturesque town near the water, was just south from the industrialized town of North Bend. It was a stone's throw away from the Cape Arago lighthouse, the beaches below, and the fishing docks. Rain was a frequent occurrence in these parts, as was fog. It was common to see the light from the lighthouse shining in the gloom to guide ships on their way. Such was the climate this February of 1921, with the promise of more rainfall and cold fronts through the month and into March.

Betty Featherwin walked down the street in Marshfield on this cool morning, rainboots on her feet and an umbrella in her hand. She had a confident air about her and walked with purpose. An orange cat named Leopold walked alongside her. He was larger than a normal cat, with thick fur, a long bushy tail, and bright green eyes. The two were heading towards a bookshop in town called The Sapphire Key. This is where Betty and the cat spent much of their time.

Betty was a young woman with long dark hair, brown eyes, and a mind that was always eager to learn. She had inherited The Sapphire Key in 1918 from her late father, Henry, after he passed from the flu[1]. Since then, she had worked tirelessly to continue his legacy and turn the

---

[1] The Spanish Influenza struck the Coos Bay area in the fall of 1918.

bookshop into a business that he would be proud of. She stayed true to this goal, and now it was arguably one of the most profitable businesses in Marshfield. Last year, Betty hired an assistant, Elizabeth Satton, to help with shop management.

The bookshop was already full of activity by the time Betty arrived. As she opened the door at a quarter past eight-o-clock, with Leopold at her heels, she saw Elizabeth standing near the front counter. She was speaking to a man in working clothes. Betty presumed that the man was the contractor they had been expecting to come by, and she soon realized that she was correct. He was due at half past eight, not a quarter past, and so he was slightly early. As Betty closed the door behind her and stepped forward to greet the contractor, she gave a grateful smile to her assistant. It was fortunate that Elizabeth had been in early to let him in. Elizabeth had proven herself, and Betty knew she could trust her to handle the various tasks involved in maintaining the bookshop.

"Good morning," Betty greeted, extending a hand to the man.

"Morning, ma'am," the man responded. "My name is George Martin. I'm a friend of Mr. Clarence Highley. He said you were in need of a contractor."

Betty beamed. Clarence Grover Highley was a good friend, and another person she could trust and rely upon. Clarence lived with his parents, John and Alice, in Marshfield. The Highleys were neighbors of Betty and her mother, Bea, and prominent residents of Coos County. Clarence was eleven years senior to Betty and was somewhat like a brother to her. He worked as an electrician at the lumbermill in North Bend, and often made visits to the bookshop. On one particular visit a year ago, Clarence had brought Leopold, the large orange cat, with him. Betty bonded with this intelligent and vocal cat. She adored him and felt that they understood each other. Leopold was part of her family and tended to accompany her everywhere.

When Betty had last spoken to Clarence, she mentioned that she might want a contractor to come by the bookshop. Clarence said that he knew a good man who worked at the lumbermill and would get in touch with him. Clarence had certainly followed through.

"It's good to meet you, Mr. Martin," Betty replied. "I've been thinking about building out to add a room to this existing space. I wondered if I could have your opinion."

Mr. Martin nodded. "Certainly. With the way this building is constructed, I can't guarantee that you can add on, but I'm happy to take a look."

"Thank you. Elizabeth, would you show Mr. Martin to the Reading Room? I'll just set my things down and join you in a moment."

Elizabeth responded, "Of course," and then headed down the hall with Mr. Martin. Leopold decided to tag along as well and hopped out in from of them. As Betty hung up her coat in the storage room, she could hear Mr. Martin laugh and remark, "Nice cat!"

Betty soon joined them in the Reading Room and felt a small stirring of excitement. Her gaze fell across the antique writing desk underneath the broad window and the corner where the back wall could possibly be built out.

"This is a nice room you have here," Mr. Martin said. "Beautiful fireplace." His eyes rested on the brick fireplace and hearth with the gaze of a skilled craftsman who had likely constructed similar hearths in the buildings nearby.

"Thank you. This is the Reading Room, where visitors come to read and relax," Betty explained. "The reason I brought you here is because this…" She moved over a step and pointed towards the back wall. "…this is where I want to put the addition."

Mr. Martin glanced at her as if to ask permission to walk over. Betty nodded, and he joined her at the back wall. After eyeing it for a moment, he pulled out of his pocket a steel measuring tape of the kind that was used at the lumbermill to measure timber. He asked, "Is there anything on the other side of this wall?"

Betty shook her head. "Just bare land."

"I've checked the permits, and we own that land extending to one acre," Elizabeth added.

"Well, good," Mr. Martin replied, turning to look at her. "That was my next question."

"What do you think?" Betty asked.

"Well, seeing as there's no obstacle on the other side, construction could easily begin on the addition. We would need to do one more check on the permits with your building plan and specifications. Once that is cleared, we would be good to go."

Betty nodded, feeling satisfied with this. "Could you give me an estimate of the timeline and cost?"

"Surely. That'll depend on the range of the project— tearing down the wall, adding a door, and building out the rest of this room. You want to make the Reading Room bigger—is that right?"

"Not exactly," Betty responded with a small smile. "I'd like this to be a separate room, attached only to this room by a glass door."

"Ah," Mr. Martin responded. He had taken a pad of paper out of his back pocket and was making notes. "That is possible. Out of curiosity," he continued, "What are you planning to make of the space?"

For a moment, Betty could see the space in its finished form, and she knew that this would be the right decision. Even if she waited a little while on the project, she knew that it was the next step to enhancing the bookshop and honoring her father's original vision for it. "The plan is to make it into a coffee shop."

Mr. Martin nodded, and continued making notes. Coffee shop additions were commonplace. Many hotels and stores in the area had their own coffee shops or cafés, which embraced the growing trend of providing full service to the customer. Mr. Martin remarked that he had overseen these types of additions before, and the work would be standard once the building permit was cleared. Betty felt even more confident that this would be a good move. She could not wait to share the news with her friends.

൫

Clarence Grover Highley stopped by with Thomas Erwinshire later in the afternoon. Clarence was on his break from work at the lumbermill. Thomas, on the other hand, kept his own schedule and could visit Betty at The Sapphire Key when he was not otherwise working.

While Betty had known Clarence her entire life, she met Thomas last year. He had come into town from Dayton, Washington. He was a publisher and owned a publishing and editing business based out of Washington called Erwinshire Publishing. His friend, Mr. Dow Isaac Ball, had spoken well of The Sapphire Key to Thomas, and encouraged him to pay a visit to the bookshop. Mr. Ball was from a respected family and happened to be a friend of Betty's family and her neighbors, the Highleys. He had suggested to Thomas that Betty's bookshop could be a potential distributor for the books that Erwinshire Publishing put into print. Thomas acted on this suggestion and met Betty, and the two began a partnership. The Sapphire Key debuted one of Erwinshire Publishing's new novels. This was fruitful and solidified their business relationship and friendship.

While getting to know each other during the book debut, Betty and Thomas realized that they had other things in common. Betty's favorite poet was a woman named May Bell Sebastian. This woman also happened to be Thomas' mother. She had died in 1897 from a devastating carriage accident when Thomas was just one year old. May Bell and Thomas' father, Phillip, had been passengers. The carriage had overturned and rolled down a hill and into a ravine. It left no survivors. May Bell Sebastian's body had been identified, but Phillip Sebastian's had not. After his parents' death, Thomas had been taken in by his mother's sister, Violet, who raised him as if he was her own child. Thomas did not learn about what happened to his parents until later in life. This bothered him, and he decided to investigate the truth about his parents and the mysterious carriage accident. Betty supported this and wanted to help him.

In a startling turn of events, Clarence's mother, Mrs. Alice Highley, gave a photograph to Betty. This photograph pictured two women standing beside each other: Mrs. Alice Highley's sister, Sarah Mitchell Mount, and May Bell Sebastian. Betty and Thomas were both amazed by this. Thomas then wrote a letter to Sarah, and recently received a response from her. Sarah explained that she had been friends with his mother and knew all about the carriage accident. She also wrote that May Bell Sebastian was buried in a cemetery in Kansas.

Thomas wished to visit his mother's gravesite and decided to take a trip to Kansas. He had invited Betty to join him, and she accepted. They had been on this journey together and would see it through to its conclusion.

In addition to making plans for the trip to Kansas, Thomas was also planning to open a second branch of Erwinshire Publishing. This involved a great deal of preparation and would not be a quick process. It required Thomas to keep up with his publishing work while he made efforts to open the new branch. To accomplish this, he rose early on most mornings to go through drafts of papers and manuscripts, and then spent a large part of the day working on other items related to his publishing business. This included reading or talking on the phone with his associates, John Noble and Charles Bunton, who worked in the main office in Washington. Working from a distance was less of a burden now that the three men had worked out a schedule between themselves. In fact, the Washington office functioned rather well with John and Charles in charge, which required less of Thomas' input and presence. This worked in Thomas' favor, especially when it came time for him to announce his intent to open a branch of Erwinshire Publishing in Coos County.

His associates had taken the news surprisingly well. Thomas recounted to Betty that, when he sprang the news on John, the reply had been, "Of course. You fell in love with that town a while ago." Thomas had laughed and said, "Well, you got me there. It has a charm that even I can't explain."

After that, Thomas had made quick work of searching for possible locations. He recently landed on a building for lease in town, about a mile away from The Sapphire Key and at the midpoint between Marshfield and North Bend. Prices in

North Bend were higher, so it made more sense to remain in Marshfield for the time being.

Thomas was staying quite busy, so Betty was pleased to see him come in with Clarence. When the two men entered the bookshop and took off their hats, she could tell that the rain had started again. She could hear the drizzle outside, and saw them brushing their feet on the doormat before coming in.

"I'll be with you in a minute," Betty called from a far bookshelf, and they waited for her by the front counter. Leopold had sensed that they were on their way a half-hour ago and scampered up to them with a cheerful meow.

"Hello," Betty heard Clarence reply. "Are we late?"

She turned the corner and headed towards them. "You're right on time," she answered with a smile.

"The rain has started again," Thomas commented. "We thought we'd go into town for coffee."

"That sounds perfect," Betty replied. "I'll get my coat and then we can go."

After Betty locked the front door of the bookshop, the three of them left for the pier in Clarence's Model-T. There was a café there that was one of their favorite spots to have a light meal and coffee. They often went midday for lunch. It was a short drive, and they arrived within a few minutes.

Clarence parked and they stepped out of the car to begin walking along the pier towards the café. Betty paused for a moment, letting Thomas and Clarence go ahead of her. She stood, with an umbrella in her hand, gazing up at the lighthouse. It had been in its place atop the cliffs for many years. Betty admired its sturdiness and wondered at the secrets that must be held within its walls. The dampness in the air made her shiver, and she drew her overcoat more snugly around herself.

"Betty," Thomas called to her. She turned her head and saw him walking quickly over to her. "Won't you come inside? You'll catch cold out here," he said, a look of concern on his face as he offered his arm to her.

"I'm coming in," Betty replied, taking his arm, and they walked into the dry and warm café. "You're right. It is cold, and I'm ready for that coffee," she added with a smile.

"Coming right up," Thomas answered, and they joined Clarence at a round table. The waitress was standing near the back counter and gave them a wave. They were all frequent customers of this café. It was one of the first places that Betty had taken Thomas, many months ago, when they had first met.

The waitress brought them cups of coffee right away. They already had lunch earlier in the afternoon. Leopold the cat was ready for a bite, however. He meowed at the waitress and looked up at her with his large eyes that made everyone fall in love with him. Betty raised her eyebrows, knowing the waitress would be bringing him a treat. He was an adored (and somewhat spoiled) cat. The three sat with their coffee and began chatting while they waited for the waitress to return with a small dish of tuna for Leopold.

Clarence asked, "So, when do you two leave for the Midwest?" and took a sip from his coffee cup.

Thomas glanced over at Betty and answered, "We're planning to go next month, in March. We'll take the train."

Clarence nodded and added, "Mother said that cousin May is looking forward to seeing you. Will you be staying with her while you're there?" May Mount-Mosier was Clarence's cousin, and Sarah Mitchell Mount's daughter. She lived in Pratt, Kansas with her husband and daughter, Florence. Betty had met May Mount-Mosier and Florence last year when they visited the Highleys and had taken an instant liking to them. When May found out that Thomas and Betty would be traveling to Kansas, she wrote and offered that they stay as guests in her home.

"Yes, I think we will, for the first part of the trip," Betty responded, and received a confirming nod from Thomas. "It was generous of her to invite us."

Thomas added that they would spend the remaining two days of their trip with Sarah Mitchell Mount, who lived in the adjacent state of Oklahoma. They would travel by passenger train along the Union Pacific railway, which was nicely outfitted with individual passenger compartments and dine-in service. When May Mount-Mosier visited Marshfield with her daughter last year, she had talked in length about the train ride and how comfortable it was. It was common for women to travel by train, and the individual compartments provided suitable accommodations. Betty was therefore confident about this manner of travel and felt comfortable about the trip.

The three of them moved on to other subjects as they finished their coffee. Betty updated them about the contractor's visit to the bookshop and plans for adding on the coffee shop. This was brilliant news, they commented, and were glad that Betty was making plans to move forward with it. A coffee shop had been part of the original plans for the bookshop and Betty had been thinking about it for some time. The timing now seemed right to explore those plans, Betty explained, though the timing of the construction was not yet set.

"That's all right," Clarence responded. "Your father would be proud to know that you're planning for it."

Betty smiled softly. Clarence had known her father, as they used to work at the lumbermill together. At that time, ten years ago, Clarence, his father, John, and Henry

Featherwin were an inseparable trio. When Henry left the lumbermill to focus on running The Sapphire Key, Clarence and John Highley stayed in touch and knew about Henry's early plans for the bookshop. Betty was touched that Clarence recalled Henry's wish to include a coffee shop in The Sapphire Key.

"Yes, I think he would be proud," Betty said, and Thomas nodded in mutual agreement.

It was pleasant to chat with one another as they warmed up and watched the rain patter against the windows. Within the hour, however, it was time to leave the café and head back into town. Clarence would drop Betty and Thomas off at The Sapphire Key and then he would drive to his home. He was finished with work at the lumbermill for the day.

⚘

It was a quick ride to the bookshop. Clarence saw them off and then waved goodbye before driving down the road.

Betty opened the door and the three of them stepped inside. The bookshop was cozy and inviting, with myrtle wood tables, sapphire-blue lamps, and bookshelves lined with books. It gave the shop a paper-and-ink scent that Betty loved. She turned to look around the shop, admiring all of the details. Apart from the contractor's visit earlier, it had been a quiet day and she had not received many customers. Her assistant, Elizabeth, had finished sorting through receipts early, and so Betty encouraged her to take the rest of the day off. It was now an hour before the shop's normal closing time. As Betty glanced around, she considered locking up early. It was a good day for it, with all of this rain. Also, she thought, it would not hurt to arrive back home a little earlier than usual. Her mother, Bea, would be happy to have Betty and Leopold on time for dinner.

"Do you plan on staying for a while?" Thomas asked, interrupting her thoughts.

"I was just thinking of closing up early, actually," she responded, looking over at him. "What do you think about that, Leopold?"

The cat gave a vocal meow, which made both Betty and Thomas smile. "I think that settles it," Betty remarked.

"I'll help you close up," Thomas offered, and began drawing the curtains.

Betty nodded gratefully. "How was your morning, by the way?" she asked as she turned down one of the sapphire-blue lamps. "I meant to ask you earlier."

"Good," he replied. "I read through a manuscript—a collection of short stories—and then I went into town to run a few errands. I didn't get caught in the rain when I was out earlier, but now, alas..." He gestured towards the steadily increasing drizzle outside.

"Rain is a certainty in Coos County," Betty replied as she drew the last set of curtains.

"It's best to make peace with it, as I often say to visitors," Thomas added.

Betty smiled. He had grown up in Washington state, so had long been used to damp weather. "Speaking of visitors, have you seen anyone around the Highley house lately?"

Betty was referring to the recent appearance of a woman at the Highley residence. Her visits had been more frequent of late, under the appearance that she was paying the Highley family a visit. This was true, except that she was visiting Clarence in particular. She had first been introduced to everyone as Ms. Inez Delzell in December, during the winter festival. At the time, it appeared that Clarence was somewhat taken with her. Thomas, in fact, had noticed this right away. He would likely know if things had progressed with the two, as he remained a regular visitor of the Highleys. He had stayed as a guest in their home for a few weeks last year when the Marshfield Inn had closed temporarily for repairs due to a small fire. He became close to the Highley family in the process and made a custom of dropping in for tea every other week. Betty was curious about Ms. Delzell and hoped to get to know her better.

"I know who you're referring to," Thomas responded with a knowing smile. "And you'll hear nothing about it from me."

"Hmm," Betty responded, with a disappointed glance in his direction. "You're bound to secrecy, then?" she added, somewhat teasingly.

"If it's anyone's secret, it's Clarence's," Thomas rejoined swiftly, and then Betty knew that Ms. Inez Delzell was definitely visiting Clarence.

"Well, I'll leave it alone," she responded. "Shall we go?"

After giving the shop a final look-over, Betty locked the door and they headed out into the damp streets. Thomas would accompany Betty and Leopold home before making his way back to the Marshfield Inn.

On the way, Betty asked Thomas how his plan to open a second branch of Erwinshire Publishing was progressing. He had kept this plan under wraps, and only Betty had known about it until just recently.

"I'm taking my time with it," Thomas responded. "I think I've found the right location," he continued, referring to the building for lease in Marshfield. "There will be more time in several months to really focus on the next steps."

"That makes sense," Betty responded.

"In the meantime, there are lots of things to keep busy with," he added.

"Oh?" Betty said with a smile, though she anticipated where Thomas was heading.

"Our trip to Kansas, for one."

"Yes," Betty nodded. Thomas had expressed how pleased he was that Betty would be on the journey with him. He appreciated her unwavering support and told her that there was no one else he would want to join him on this quest to discover the truth about his parents. This expression of emotion had surprised her a bit, though also warmed her heart. She too could not imagine it any other way, as she had been on this journey with him from the beginning.

"There will certainly be enough to do leading up to the trip," Betty continued.

"Yes, and I'm looking forward to it. I hope you are as well," Thomas responded. They had reached the Featherwin house and stood by the porch.

"Well," Betty stepped forward to whisper. "It will be a little hard to leave Leopold behind, but I think he'll manage." The cat would stay behind with Betty's mother, Bea, and would have the freedom to come and go as he pleased. Betty had a sense that he would be fine and knew he would receive a lot of attention from Elizabeth while they were gone. "And yes, I am looking forward to the trip very much."

Thomas smiled and reached forward to brush away a strand of hair that had fallen across her face and drew his hand away just as quickly. "I'm glad," he murmured. "And this is where I leave you." He stepped back a pace and said, "Good night."

"Good night, then, and I'll see you tomorrow," Betty replied, and her hand unconsciously drifted to the spot behind her ear where he had brushed the strand of her hair. He turned to head down the street towards the Inn.

Leopold meowed at her, and Betty opened the door to let them inside and out of the rain. They were immediately greeted by Bea, Betty's mother. She was wearing an apron, and by the smells that were wafting from the kitchen, she was in the midst of preparing dinner.

"Was that Mr. Erwinshire?" Bea asked, helping Betty out of her coat.

"It was."

"Fine young man," Bea commented.

Betty smiled. Her mother, and many others in town, liked Thomas and thought he was a respectable young man. Betty, of course, liked him as well. Their friendship had blossomed over the past few months. She cared about him, and she knew that he cared about her too. "Yes, he is," she responded.

"I'm glad you're home, as I've just made dinner," Bea continued.

"It smells good," Betty commented. "And I hope you saved some for Leopold," she added, with a soft laugh. Leopold was already heading towards the kitchen, sniffing the air and licking his lips.

"Yes, I did," Bea replied. "I know I always say this, but he is one spoiled cat."

Betty laughed, and the two of them followed Leopold into the kitchen to enjoy a warm and cozy dinner.

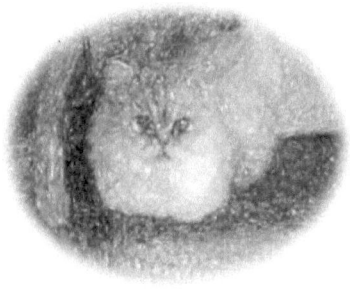

Chapter 2

Dinner & Dessert

The following day at the bookshop passed by quickly. After the brief lull that came in January after the holidays, business had picked up again. Saturdays, especially, were busier days. Many of the locals came by with their children on Saturday, and shoppers from North Bend visited the bookshop as well. Recently, Betty had seen an increase in younger readers. They brought a bright, positive energy into The Sapphire Key and enjoyed petting Leopold while they looked through the fiction bookshelves. Among these youthful shoppers was a young man named Ernest. He had come into The Sapphire Key in January to drop off a letter and had never been inside of a bookshop before. His enthusiasm had heartened Betty, and she allowed him to take any book he wanted as a gift. Since then, Ernest had stopped by several times and brought a couple of his friends with him.

Betty sometimes wondered whether the increase in her younger customers was because of Ernest, Leopold, or her book inventory, or all three. Whatever the case, it made her smile. She hoped that these younger folks would develop an appreciation for reading, just as she had when she was young, and her father introduced her to the world of books.

"Well, it has been a busy day," Elizabeth Satton, Betty's assistant, commented. She stood by the Fiction bookshelf, counting the number of duplicate book copies.

"Yes, it has," Betty agreed. "I was pleased to see Ernest come by again with his friend."

Elizabeth looked over at Betty and smiled. "Me too. You predicted that he would become one of our regular customers."

Betty laughed softly and nodded at the remembrance. "I'm glad the prediction came true."

She walked over to the front counter, where she had placed a copy of the novel *On the Level* by T.Y.L. in between two matching myrtle wood bookends. The book, and the book ends, made her think of Thomas Erwinshire. *On the Level* had been published by Erwinshire Publishing last year, and Betty had promoted it in The Sapphire Key. It was the reason Betty had met Thomas in the first place. When Betty made his acquaintance—courtesy of their mutual friend, Mr. Dow Isaac Ball—Thomas had been in search of a potential distributor for the new novel. He had asked Betty to consider it. She did and was so pleased with the quality of the novel that she agreed to partner with Erwinshire Publishing and promote the book. The novel, which presented a fictionalized account of the sport of baseball during the 1890s, was immensely popular. The subject of the novel happened to interest many people, and sales exceeded Betty's expectations. Many locals, including the lumbermill workers, loved to play baseball and enjoyed the novel's portrayal of the game and the players. Betty went through two shipments of the book due to the demand for it and had filled a number of order requests. One order request even came from Mr. L.J. Simpson, who was well-known as the founder and former mayor of North Bend and as the owner of many enterprises in the Coos Bay area.[2]

The bookends had been a Christmas gift from Thomas. They were carved from tan and chestnut-colored myrtle wood, the most common type of timber in Coos County.

---

[2] Louis Jerome Simpson was indeed the real-life founder and mayor of North Bend, Oregon, and lived on a sprawling estate called Shore Acres on the cliffs of Coos Bay.

Thomas spent several weekends crafting them, and had even etched cats on each, with clear markings for the ears, nose, and whiskers. He had also embedded small, jade-colored stones into the wood for the cats' eyes. The cats were intended to represent Leopold. It was beautiful work and Betty smiled every time she looked at them.

She smiled now as she approached the front counter and reached to take the novel, *On the Level*, out from between the bookends. The novel had a sturdy, deep brown cover, and the title and author's name were printed in navy blue lettering. As she drew her hand over the lettering, she said to Elizabeth, "Have we had any more requests for *On the Level* lately?"

Elizabeth had crouched down to place a book on a bottom shelf and returned to standing to respond to Betty. "In fact, we have."

Betty's eyes drifted up to look at Elizabeth in pleasant surprise. "That's good to hear."

Elizabeth nodded. "The bookshop in Pasco was running low on inventory, so some customers decided to order from us instead."

"I see," Betty remarked. The novel had been placed in several bookstores for distribution, including one in Pasco, Washington. From what Thomas had told her, distribution would expand to other bookstores over the next few months. In the meantime, Marshfield, Oregon and Pasco, Washington were the sole west coast distributors. This accounted for the high sales of the novel at The Sapphire Key. Sales would level out once more bookstores stocked the novel.

"I don't think we will need to order another shipment. We have a good number of copies still," Elizabeth continued. She kept track of book requests and inventory, which was a huge help to Betty.

"Good," Betty responded, and returned the book to its place in between the bookends. This was her copy, signed by the author himself.

"Do you think we'll be busy in March?" Elizabeth asked.

Before Betty could reply, Leopold meowed loudly as he hopped down from his cushion underneath the phonograph (his usual sleeping place). He made a point of stretching out long in front of them, showing off his fiery orange fur, before trotting over to Elizabeth.

Elizabeth smiled and knelt to stroke him. "Am I to take that as "yes", Mr. Leopold?" she asked. Her fondness for him was clear in her voice. The cat purred in response.

Betty walked over to join them. Leopold flopped over on his side to reveal his large, fluffy belly. This is how he showed his contentment.

"I certainly hope we'll be busy," Betty answered. "And you will be fine."

Elizabeth glanced over at Betty with a glimmer of uncertainty in her eyes. "I will do my best."

"Of course, you will," Betty responded. "I have no doubt that you can handle everything while I'm gone," she said to reassure Elizabeth. "And remember, it's just for a couple of weeks." She and Thomas would be in Kansas in March, visiting May Bell Sebastian's gravesite and visiting with Sarah Mitchell Mount and her daughter. Betty had prepared to entrust The Sapphire Key to Elizabeth's care while she was away. She had also entrusted Leopold's care to her mother, Bea, though had not found the heart to break the news to Leopold yet.

"Yes, you're right," Elizabeth said as she rose to her feet. "I'll make sure the shop stays in good shape."

Betty nodded, feeling confident in her assistant.

"Are you looking forward to the trip?"

At that moment, their conversation was interrupted by the bell on the front door jangling. They both looked towards the front of the shop and saw Mr. James Smithson standing in the doorway. James was one of Betty's dear friends, and the brother of her best friend, Edith. He worked at the lumbermill and lived in North Bend.

"James," she smiled, and approached to greet him.

"Good evening, Betty. Good evening, Elizabeth," he greeted, lowering the brim of his hat. "I was driving this way and thought I would stop in and say hello."

"That was good of you. We're pleased to see you," Elizabeth responded. James smiled as she came forward.

"Would you like to sit?" Betty asked.

"Oh, no, I can't stay long," James replied, with a glance at Elizabeth. "And, you'll be closing up soon."

As James spoke, Betty glanced down at her wristwatch. She was startled to see that it was half past five. *My, the day has just flown by!* she thought. "You're welcome to stay for a bit," she still offered. She was pleased to receive customers past closing time, and even more pleased to receive her friends.

"No, thank you. I just wanted to say hello. I'll help you close up, if you like," James replied, and glanced again at Elizabeth.

Betty smiled. "That is kind of you."

"I'll turn down the lamps, and James, could you draw the curtains?" Elizabeth asked. James nodded in response. This only left locking the Reading Room door and checking the storage room.

Betty set off to do that, looking over at James and Elizabeth in appreciation. She thought about how kind it was for James to stop in and then offer to help. It was nice to have such good friends. After she turned the key to lock the Reading Room door, and started walking towards the storage room, she heard James and Elizabeth's voices. She did not intend to listen to their conversation, but she overheard them.

"...I enjoyed the hayride. It was a nice winter festival."

"Yes, it was."

"I'm glad you came by afterwards. It was such fun making that tree out of books."

They were speaking about the winter festival this past December. Afterwards, James had come by the bookshop with his mother, Ruth, to take a look at their holiday window display. Betty remembered that James had joked that they should add a tree made from books to the display. The next day, Elizabeth had surprised Betty with just that. Betty had assumed that Elizabeth had placed the books in the shape of a Christmas tree herself. By James and Elizabeth's conversation, however, it sounded like James may have helped her.

"I was wondering if, perhaps, you'd like to join me for dinner," James was saying.

Upon hearing this, Betty quickly entered the storage room to gather her belongings. She did not hear the remainder of their conversation. When she joined them again, they were standing near the front door and chatting about how large Leopold was.

"Thank you for helping," Betty remarked to them. "We're ready to go."

The two nodded, and then they all headed out for the evening. Betty, Elizabeth, and Leopold saw James to his car, and then went on their way down the street. Elizabeth said nothing about her conversation with James, but instead told

Betty of her plans to update The Sapphire Key's catalogue of books. Betty remarked that this was a good time to update the catalogue, and James and Elizabeth's conversation drifted out of her mind.

She would be home soon and must get ready for dinner. She was expecting Thomas to stop by. They would be going over their travel plans. This was at the front of her mind lately, as it should be.

Cઢ

Thomas was expected at the Featherwin house at six-o-clock for dinner. When the hour arrived, but he had not, Betty supposed that work had held him up. She chatted with her mother in the meantime.

Bea was in the kitchen, finishing up dinner preparations. She had baked cranberry muffins to serve alongside the main dish. Betty took the basket of muffins into the dining room and passed Leopold on the way. The large, orange cat sat in the doorway of the kitchen. He had a red toy bird in between his paws and looked very content. Betty had given the bird to Leopold as a Christmas gift last year. He loved to carry it as he followed Betty and Bea around the house. The sight of him with the toy bird in his mouth always brought a smile to Betty's face.

"Thank you for inviting Thomas to stay for dinner," Betty commented, as she placed the basket on the table.

"Of course," Bea replied. "Your friends are always welcome. And I look forward to hearing more about your travel plans."

Betty nodded. "It is amazing how time has flown—we leave in two weeks."

Bea smiled and looked at Betty with a thoughtful expression. "Time has passed quickly, and you've had a great year." She paused and placed a hand on her daughter's arm. "Your father would be proud of you—I certainly am."

"Oh, mother," Betty said softly, and stood to embrace her. "Thank you, that means a lot." Bea gave Betty another smile and told her that she was also glad for Thomas.

In January, after he had received the letter from Sarah Mitchell Mount, Thomas told Bea about his parents and his desire to learn more about them. Bea understood how important it would be for him to visit his mother's gravesite in Kansas. It was about remembering family. She supported Thomas in his decision to make the trip. She also felt it would be nice for Betty to accompany him. Bea knew Alice Highley well, and was familiar with her relatives, Sarah Mitchell Mount and May Mount-Mosier. She was also familiar with the area that Thomas and Betty would be traveling to. Her late husband, Henry Featherwin, had family throughout the midwestern states, including Missouri and Oklahoma. She felt comfortable that Thomas and Betty would be among good people. She also hoped that they would be able to visit some of Henry's extended family during the trip. Betty had seen very little of her midwestern Featherwin relatives and would love to visit them. She knew that this would make her mother happy. She and Thomas had promised to try their best to see the Oklahoma Featherwins too.

Betty told her mother that she was excited for the trip. She looked forward to sharing more of their plans once Thomas arrived. Betty then began updating Bea about her day. In the midst of this conversation, there was a knock at the front door.

Betty glanced at her watch and saw that it was a quarter past six-o-clock. "That must be Thomas," she remarked.

When she walked towards the front door, Leopold was already pawing at the door. Betty glanced at him fondly. He was a smart and intuitive cat. He always knew when visitors were on their way before she did.

She opened the door to let their guest inside. Thomas lowered the brim of his hat as he entered. He immediately uttered an apology for being late. Betty and Bea did not mind, as they were just pleased to have him over for dinner. Still, Thomas went on to explain the reason for the slight delay.

"I was just leaving the Inn…" Thomas began, as he placed his hat and coat on the coatrack. "…when I had an unexpected visitor."

"Oh?" Betty responded curiously.

"It was an old friend from college, who I haven't seen in years," Thomas continued. They began walking down the hall towards the dining room. "Happened to be in town for the day and stopped by to say hello."

"Oh, how nice," Betty replied. "Did you have any time to catch up with your friend?"

"Not much, but that's all right," Thomas responded with a smile. "I was looking forward to joining you both for dinner."

"We are so pleased to have you," Bea said, and showed him to a seat at the dining table. "Please sit, and let's eat while the food is warm," she suggested. "Will you have time to stay for tea after dinner?"

Thomas said that he would be glad to stay for tea, and they began enjoying the meal. Bea and Thomas chatted, and then the three of them went on to discuss Thomas and Betty's travel plans.

"The Mounts are all very kind and welcoming," Bea said. Thomas and Betty had confirmed that they would be staying with May Mount-Mosier while in Kansas, and then with

Sarah Mitchell Mount in Oklahoma. "Did you know that Sarah Mount has eight children?"

Betty and Thomas shook their heads.

"May is her daughter, of course. She also has a boy named Joseph, who must be sixteen years old now. Her other children are scattered across the states," Bea continued. "Maybe you'll meet Joseph while you're at Sarah's house."

Betty nodded and smiled. It was interesting to hear about Mrs. Alice Highley's other family members. "Yes," she responded. "It will be nice to meet Mrs. Highley's relatives."

Thomas nodded in agreement. He enjoyed hearing about these individuals, especially because they were part of a large family. To Thomas, the Highleys and the Mounts were fascinating because they represented a sense of family that he never had. He sometimes wondered what his life would be like if his parents had survived and raised him. He felt, somehow, that getting to know the Mounts would bring him closer to getting to know his parents. He would be learning about the Mounts while on a journey to learn about his own family. This made the trip to the Midwest even more wonderful and meaningful to him.

"Betty told me that you have family in that area as well," he added.

Bea nodded and proceeded to tell him about the Featherwins. Many people had migrated from the Midwest to Oregon and California in the 1800s for work. There were ample opportunities in the lumber and shipbuilding business. Henry, and the Highleys, had followed opportunity to Coos Bay. Some of the other Featherwins (like some of the Mounts) chose to stay in the Midwest for farming.

"I'm sure you're eager to find more information about your parents," Bea commented.

"Yes, I am," Thomas replied. He glanced over at Betty and said, "Thank you for your support."

Betty smiled softly. "Absolutely."

"Have you told your family about the trip?" Bea asked. Betty looked over at Bea and wondered how Thomas would respond to her question. Thomas had told Bea that his Aunt Violet had raised him. He had not told Bea that his relationship with the Erwinshires had become strained in the recent years, however.

"No, I have not," Thomas responded quietly. "We are not very close, I'm afraid," he continued. "My Aunt Violet hid the truth about what happened to my parents. She never wished to talk about my mother." His eyes drifted towards Betty, and she looked at him reassuringly. "I still don't know her reasons, and I admit that it bothers me," he continued. "I do not feel that she would support my efforts to learn about my parents."

Betty's face flushed slightly as he said this. She was reminded of the letter from Violet Erwinshire to Thomas, which she had tucked away in her bedroom drawer. Thomas had never opened the letter. Instead, Betty saw that he had tossed the envelope into the trash can at The Sapphire Key. It was clear that he did not want to know its contents. When he was gone, she took the envelope out of the trash, brought it home with her, and (in a moment where curiosity overcame her restraint) she opened it and read it. And then, she read it again. Betty had never met Violet Erwinshire. After reading the letter, she never cared to meet her. Thomas was correct to discard it, she thought. The letter would be devastating to him.

Betty was lost in her thoughts and missed Bea's response to Thomas. By the time she joined in the conversation again, they had moved on to a different topic.

Betty took a sip of water and relaxed. No one knew about Violet Erwinshire's letter, and that was the way it should be. Betty resolved to make sure it stayed a secret.

⁌

The evening ended on a pleasant note. They all retired to the parlor with tea after dinner and chatted idly for another half hour before Thomas departed. He thanked them for their hospitality and promised to see Betty and Leopold at The Sapphire Key the following day.

The moment Thomas stepped foot outside the Featherwin house, his thoughts turned to his unexpected visitor. It had indeed been an old friend from college. Thomas had not told Betty and Bea that his friend was a young woman named Audrey Wilson. Furthermore, Thomas was once engaged to be married to her. They had been seeing each other for just a short while and were engaged for just a few weeks. It was a college romance. Thomas had broken it off, and they parted ways as friends. This occurred over two years ago, and Thomas had not spoken to or seen Audrey Wilson at all during that time. Her visit was a surprise, to put it mildly, and Thomas did not know how to react when he saw her. All he knew, for sure, was that he had agreed to have dinner with Audrey before he hurried out of the Inn to go have dinner with the Featherwins.

Walking back to the Inn now, he mulled over his decision. He believed that it was inappropriate to discuss previous relationships, and therefore he had never told Betty about Audrey. It was best to keep that in the past, he thought. At the same time, he thought it would not cause any harm to have dinner with Audrey as old friends. He decided, as he entered his room at the Inn, that there was no reason to tell

Betty about it. He would go ahead and meet Audrey for dinner before she returned to Washington, and that would be all.

ଓଃ

Meanwhile, Betty and Bea tidied the kitchen and got ready to turn in for the night. Bea felt that it had been a nice evening. She reminded Betty that she would be doing laundry the next day and asked Betty to give her any clothing that needed to be cleaned. Betty said that she would and placed a couple of blouses into the laundry basket. She would put those, in addition to other items, in her luggage for the trip to Kansas.

When she went into her bedroom with Leopold, she immediately walked over to her bedside table. She opened the drawer and took out a white envelope. It was addressed to Thomas Erwinshire. The return address on the upper left-hand corner stated, "Violet Erwinshire". Betty remembered the contents of the letter so vividly that she did not need to read it again. The written words still echoed in her mind.

Pursing her lips, she looked down at the envelope. She could not take it back to the bookshop, and she did not want to destroy it. She wanted to hide it and banish it from her mind. Not able to think of anything else in the moment, she decided to put it in her dresser drawer underneath some clothing. That was a place no one else would look.

She quietly walked over to the dresser. Pulling open the drawer, she lifted several folded garments inside and tucked the envelope underneath. She closed the drawer again and sighed. Now it was hidden, and it need never cross her mind again.

Leopold meowed at her inquiringly. She returned to the bed and sat down next to the cat to pet him. "We all have secrets, Leopold," she whispered. "This is just one of them."

∽

Mrs. Violet Erwinshire
Dayton, Washington
December 15, 1920

Dear Thomas,
I hope this letter finds you well. I am sorry we did not get to see you on Thanksgiving. I know you were not happy last year during the holiday. You had many questions about your birth mother. As far as I'm concerned, I <u>am</u> your mother. I raised you. I changed your last name from Sebastian to Erwinshire because you were my baby. You did not need to know your real last name.
When I finally told you something about your mother (my sister), I immediately regretted it. I was never able to have a child of my own, and with you, I had one. When my sister died, I could finally be a mother. It was all I had ever wanted, and all I could think about. My concern had to be you; anything else that had happened was unimportant to me. I just wanted to hold a baby in my arms.
There were many things I could have told you about your parents, but I chose not to. You are an Erwinshire. You were never a Sebastian, and you never will be.

Sincerely,

Your Mother.

Chapter 3

Restaurant Sightings

On Thursday evening, Betty was getting ready to close up the bookshop. It had been a busy day; she and Elizabeth had even worked through lunch to assist some customers. Betty had been expecting Thomas to come by, but he sent over a note stating that he had work to finish. She thus planned to stay a little while to organize a bookshelf before heading home with Leopold.

Elizabeth, meanwhile, told Betty about her plan to meet a friend for dinner in North Bend. Her friend, a young woman named Daphne, was from out-of-town. She was staying for a couple of days at the hotel in North Bend and had arrived by train. Elizabeth would be meeting her at a restaurant close to the hotel.

She was looking forward to the dinner. Daphne was a longtime friend, and they had a lot to catch up on. Betty was pleased to hear this and wished her a nice time. She said goodbye and listened to the bell on the front door rattle as Elizabeth stepped out to enjoy her evening.

CB

The Sapphire Key was calm and quiet. Leopold was curled up on his cushion under the phonograph, purring softly. It was pleasant to be in the bookshop in the evening, after everything had quieted down. The bookshop had a soothing atmosphere. The scent of paper and ink danced in the air, and the sapphire lamps turned a deeper shade of blue. Betty immediately felt peaceful as she looked at the lamps. With a small smile, she began to organize one of the bookshelves. Everything felt right in her world, and she could not imagine that anything could disrupt her contentment.

❧

The restaurant in North Bend was a popular spot. All of the tables were filled, and the waiters were rushing about to take customers' orders. Many young ladies were seated together, talking and laughing with men who might be their beaus or husbands. Everyone was smartly dressed. Some ladies even wore party dresses and sparkling jewelry. They would be sitting for a quick dinner before going to the music hall.

Elizabeth was in high spirits as she entered the restaurant with her friend, Daphne. They took in the liveliness of the restaurant and eagerly waited for the host to seat them. Daphne told her that the train ride had been very smooth, except for two young children who kept sneaking into her compartment. They were siblings and were playing hide-and-seek to occupy themselves. Daphne did not mind the disruption, and even enjoyed watching the children play.

Elizabeth smiled and laughed in response. "It sounds like those children had fun." She looked up to see the host coming towards them. "Oh, good," she commented to Daphne. "I think we'll be seated soon."

As she looked around the room, her eyes rested on a table near the back of the restaurant. She thought she recognized one of the people sitting there. She blinked and looked again.

It was Thomas Erwinshire. He was seated at a slight angle, with his face turned away, so he could not see

Elizabeth from where she and Daphne were standing. As Elizabeth continued to look, she noticed that he was sitting with an attractive young woman. They seemed to be deep in conversation, and it appeared that Thomas' hand was on top of the young woman's hand. Elizabeth felt that she should not be looking at them and moved her eyes away. As the host offered to seat them, Elizabeth asked if they could have a table in the back on the opposite side of the restaurant. She did not want Thomas to see her.

The host responded, "Of course," and they followed him to a table.

They proceeded to have a lovely dinner and slipped out of the restaurant before Thomas and the young woman. Daphne was leaving on the noon train the following day. She suggested that they have breakfast together before she headed for the train station. Elizabeth agreed. She enjoyed coming up to North Bend, and there would be plenty of time to have breakfast before she needed to open the bookshop. In addition, transportation was easy with the bus that traveled between Marshfield and North Bend throughout the day. Elizabeth could easily catch the bus to and from the restaurant.[3]

---

[3] Buses were a common mode of transportation throughout Oregon in the early 1900s. The bus, or stage line service, was a type of passenger carrier that people used to go from town to town directly. Railroad transportation was often indirect and included layovers, whereas buses offered direct routes that took much less time. The bus that Elizabeth Satton takes likely would be similar to the Gorst and King open-air bus that traveled between North Bend and Marshfield. *See* the text *Bus Transportation, Volume 2,* originally published in 1923 by McGraw-Hill, and the book *North*

Elizabeth accompanied Daphne to her hotel, and the two made a plan to meet at the restaurant again in the morning. Elizabeth then caught the last evening bus to return to Marshfield. On the way, she thought about what she had seen in the restaurant. Thomas had definitely been dining with a woman who Elizabeth did not know. It made her a little uncomfortable, though she was not sure why. The woman could be anyone—a friend or a relative—and Elizabeth was sure that their meeting had been completely innocent. She shook her head to erase it from her mind, and instead thought about how wonderful it was to catch up with Daphne.

؃

Thomas, unaware that Elizabeth had just left, sat in the same restaurant with his unexpected visitor from the other day, Audrey Wilson. She was a striking woman, with bright blue eyes and blond curled hair styled in a bun. Her skin was fair, and she wore an easy smile on her face. Her attractiveness and pleasant demeanor were easily noticed by others.

That was certainly what Thomas noticed when he first met her in college. At that time, two-and-a-half years ago, Thomas had been studying English and was taking a class on the representation of art in literature. Ms. Audrey Wilson was taking the class as well. She was studying Art with a plan to become a teacher at the local elementary school. Thomas thought she was pleasant and friendly. They got to know one

---

Bend by Dick and Judy Wagner for more information (Arcadia Pub., 2010).

another while they attended the class and started meeting after class for coffee. As the months passed, their friendship deepened. Thomas appreciated Audrey's passion for art, and her perspective on some of the paintings they studied in class. He also found her enthusiasm to strike out and do something on her own refreshing. Her father was a local lawyer in Washington who handled contractual matters; her mother stayed at home. Her parents had wanted her to settle down, but she decided that she would take a teaching position after college. She had told Thomas that she liked to stay busy, and she liked art, so teaching would be perfect.

During that time, Thomas also met his friend and eventual business partner, John Noble. The three of them spent many afternoons having lunch together and discussing their post-graduation plans. One afternoon, John did not join Thomas and Audrey. Thomas had an enjoyable conversation with her and realized how much he liked her company. He thought about how nice it would be to always have these conversations. He asked Audrey, then and there, if she would marry him. To his surprise, she accepted.

The giddiness from that afternoon faded within a couple of weeks, and soon lost its novelty. Thomas began to think that his decision to marry Audrey had been premature. He liked her very much, but he was not sure if that would support marriage. He also wanted to concentrate on starting his business with John.

Thomas met with Audrey several weeks after he had proposed and broke off the engagement. Audrey merely wished him well with no hard feelings and hoped they could remain friends. Thomas promised to stay in touch, and the two of them went on with their lives. He opened Erwinshire Publishing with John Noble, and Audrey took a teaching position. They gradually lost touch, and Thomas all but forgot about her.

He remembered everything again when he saw her standing in the lobby of the Marshfield Inn. She had greeted him happily and said she was glad to see him. When Thomas asked what brought her to Marshfield, she said that she had paid a visit to Erwinshire Publishing and spoken to John. Apparently, John had told her that Thomas was in Marshfield. She had taken the next train from Washington to Oregon and was staying at the hotel in North Bend. She suggested that Thomas meet her for dinner so that they could catch up. At that point, Thomas had glanced at his watch and realized he was late for his dinner with the Featherwins. He quickly agreed to have dinner with Audrey on another night and left the Inn as quickly as he could after making sure she had a ride to North Bend.

Sitting with Audrey in the restaurant felt somewhat like old times to Thomas. She was still the same pleasant and friendly young woman. They spoke about their mutual friends from college (including John), and Thomas told her things were going well with Erwinshire Publishing. Audrey was still teaching art at a school in Pasco and would be taking additional art classes. Her news was that the classes were held in New York, so she would be traveling there soon. Thomas was happy for her, as he knew she had always wanted to travel. It was at this moment that he said,

"That's wonderful news. I'm so pleased for you, Audrey," and placed his hand briefly on top of hers.

For the remainder of dinner, Thomas updated Audrey on what had brought him to Marshfield. He told her about finding a bookshop in town as a distributor for one of the books he published. He also told her that he had made many friends and had grown very fond of the woman who owned the bookshop. Audrey smiled and expressed that she was happy for him.

The dinner seemed to pass by quickly, and Audrey said how much she enjoyed catching up. She told Thomas that she would be taking the next evening's train back to Washington and asked if there was a chance they could meet again. Without giving it much thought, Thomas suggested that they meet for breakfast. Thomas felt that it would be nice to have one more meal together before saying goodbye and wishing Audrey well. Audrey agreed, and the two parted ways.

On his way back to the Marshfield Inn, Thomas thought about how nice it was to talk to Audrey. He was pleased that she was doing well. She liked to travel, and Thomas was happy that she now had the opportunity to take classes in New York. As he considered this, he realized that it had been the right decision to break off his engagement to her. Audrey had her own life, and her own dreams. He was glad that she was following her path, just as Thomas was following his own path. His dreams had brought him to Marshfield, Oregon, and to Betty Featherwin, and he was grateful about that.

As he turned in for the night, he thought about his plans for the following day. He would have breakfast with Audrey, and then would get some work done before stopping by The Sapphire Key. His heart skipped as he thought about the bookshop, and about seeing Betty. He had not told her about the dinner with Audrey, or about breakfast. This made him a little uncomfortable, though he was not sure why. While he had a relationship with Audrey at one time, that was long past, and she was now just a friend.

He resolved not to tell Betty. There was no need to share this history, and he saw no point in recounting his past about

Audrey. He turned down the lamp and settled in to sleep for the night.

଼ଃ

The following morning, Thomas was driving to North Bend and thinking about the work he needed to accomplish during the day. He had a lot of reading to finish, and some correspondence to complete. He would have a nice breakfast with Audrey and wish her well before she caught the train back to Washington. He would then spend a large part of the day on these tasks.

It did not take him long to arrive at the restaurant, which was next door to the hotel. He easily found a place to park his car along the curb in front. As he exited the car, he saw that Audrey had just arrived as well. She smiled at him as he walked up to her, and the two of them entered the restaurant. They were seated right away, and the waitress brought them fresh coffee and a menu.

଼ଃ

Elizabeth's bus arrived early in North Bend, so she went over to the hotel to meet her friend, Daphne. The two of them walked together to the restaurant to have breakfast. As soon as they came inside, Elizabeth looked around to find a table. She started to take a step towards the coffee counter but stopped in her tracks when she saw Thomas. He was sitting at a table near the back with the same woman he had been dining with the night before. He had his back to Elizabeth, though she could easily recognize him.

Elizabeth returned to stand with Daphne at the front of the restaurant and waited to be seated. When the host arrived, she again requested to sit on the opposite side of the restaurant so that she would not be seen by Thomas. She was visibly troubled by seeing him again, and Daphne noticed.

"Elizabeth, are you all right?" Daphne asked as they sat down. "You look as though something is bothering you."

Elizabeth glanced up at her friend and smiled. "Oh, it's just something I forgot for work. It's not important, and I can get it later," she replied, and quickly changed the subject.

They had a nice breakfast. Daphne promised to visit again soon, and to write to Elizabeth in the meantime. Elizabeth said goodbye to her in the hotel lobby, and then caught the bus back to Marshfield.

During the bus ride, she decided that she would not discuss who she saw in the restaurant.

ભ

After Elizabeth left, Daphne learned that her afternoon train was delayed, and she would need to take the evening train. She spent the remainder of the day leisurely and checked out of the hotel in early evening.

She arrived at the train station on time and started to board the train. It was not crowded, and she was able to find a seat in a front compartment. She sat near an attractive woman who appeared to be around the same age as she was. As they waited for the train to depart, they started a conversation.

"Hello," the attractive woman said to Daphne. "My name is Audrey. I was just in Marshfield visiting an old friend from college. He runs his own publishing business out of Washington but has done some work here too."

"Oh, how lovely," Daphne replied, and told the woman her name. "I was visiting with a friend also. She actually works at the only bookshop in Marshfield. The owner of the bookshop is so nice. She and my friend manage the shop together."

Audrey listened intently as Daphne told her story.

Chapter 4

Folding Laundry

The morning dawned bright, with thin shafts of sunlight
streaming through the grey clouds. This hint of sunlight
lasted only one hour before the February rain returned in
full force.

Betty glanced out the window as she was preparing to
go to the bookshop, and murmured, "I hope the weather will
be a little less severe in Kansas." She and Thomas would be
leaving in a week and had timed the trip during a mild
season. In March, they were unlikely to encounter heavy
rains or storms.

As she closed the curtain, Leopold meowed at her. She
looked at him and saw something like curiosity in his green
eyes. She had not told him that he would be staying home
while she and Thomas were away. She suspected that he
already knew that, however. He was a very perceptive cat,
and Betty felt that he had an extraordinary ability to
communicate and understand her.

She knelt and rubbed behind his ears. "I know you'll
have fun with mother and Elizabeth," she told him. "You
will watch out for them, won't you?" He purred in response
and pressed his forehead against her hand. He was not only
a communicative cat, but also a protector. When there had
been a fire at the Marshfield Inn last year, he had alerted
the North Bend firemen by showing up at the fire station.
Then, he had accompanied Thomas to the Inn and stayed
with him until the danger had passed. He was a very special
cat and Betty was happy he had come into her life. She knew
he would be fine, and he would make sure Bea was fine too.

"Well, let's go to the bookshop," she said and stood to open the front door. The both of them headed out and walked side by side on their way to The Sapphire Key to start this new day.

ଔ

Elizabeth was already at the bookshop by the time Betty and Leopold arrived. She was arranging books in the shopfront window. For the month of March, they were showcasing poetry. The centerpiece was a collection of poems by Robert Frost called, *Mountain Interval.*[4] Betty smiled as she entered the shop and gazed at the book of poems. Frost was a poet she personally admired. There was something about his writing style that drew her in. He incorporated nature in his poems and created vivid images. May Bell Sebastian's poetry had a similar effect on Betty.

As she set down her shoulder bag and keys on the counter, she wished that she had a copy of May Bell's poetry to showcase. This would have been such a lovely tribute to her talent as a poet. It would have been nice for Thomas to see his mother appreciated in this way, too.

Elizabeth looked up from her task to greet Betty and noticed her expression.

"Good morning, Betty," she said. "What do you think of the window display?"

"You did a great job, Elizabeth," Betty replied with a smile. "It looks perfect. I was just wishing we had one more collection of poems to add."

---

[4] Robert Frost was an accomplished poet of the 20th century. *Mountain Interval* was one of his many poem collections. It was originally published in 1916 and republished in 1921.

Elizabeth looked at her questioningly, to which Betty responded, "May Bell Sebastian's poems."

"Oh, yes," Elizabeth said. She knew that May Bell was Betty's favorite poet. She also recently found out that May Bell was Thomas' mother. Thomas and Betty had updated Elizabeth on this history a little while ago.

"I agree that her poems would be the perfect touch. Maybe you'll come across a copy when you're in Kansas."

"I hope so," Betty responded, feeling happy at the thought. "In the meantime, let's get ready for our customers."

Elizabeth nodded, looked over the window display once more, and then joined Betty at the counter.

"By the way," Betty commented as she straightened a stack of papers, "How was your dinner last night?"

Elizabeth froze for a moment. The image of Thomas sitting in the restaurant with the young woman flashed in her mind. She quickly recovered and turned her thoughts to the time she spent with Daphne. "It was great. I loved catching up with my friend, Daphne. We chatted all through dinner."

"Oh, I'm glad. It sounds like a good evening."

Elizabeth nodded, "Yes, it was."

Betty gave her another smile, and then told her she was going into the storage room to hang her coat on the coatrack. Elizabeth nodded and remained at the counter. As Betty walked down the hall, Elizabeth let out a soft sigh. Betty gave no indication that she knew about Thomas being in the restaurant. Elizabeth recalled her decision not to mention her sighting to anyone, and she intended to stick to that decision.

The bell on the door sounded, drawing Elizabeth away from her thoughts. She stepped forward to greet their first customer of the day. "Hello, Ernest. How nice to see you. What are you in the mood to read today?"

ⓒ

Thomas got a head start on his work after meeting with Audrey for a brief, though pleasant, breakfast. They had chatted about her upcoming trip to New York, which would be the start of a new chapter in her life. Then, they wished each other well and said goodbye as they exited the restaurant. Thomas did not think that he would see her again. Walking away from her and towards Marshfield felt like the close of one chapter and the start of another in his own life.

This feeling followed him as he made his way to The Sapphire Key in late afternoon. As he paused at the threshold before opening the door, he felt his spirits lift. He was looking forward to seeing Betty and Leopold. In that moment, he realized how important they both were in his life.

Thomas reached for the door handle at the same time that Elizabeth reached for it on the other side of the door. The sensation startled them, and there was a brief moment of awkwardness as they both stepped back from the door. Thomas moved first, stepping aside to allow Elizabeth to pass. As she did, he smiled and said, "Hello, Elizabeth."

She gave him a quick smile, then lowered her eyes and hurried past him. He considered this to be somewhat out of the ordinary, as Elizabeth usually stopped to say hello whenever he came by the bookshop. He supposed that she was just in a hurry. In any case, the encounter evaporated from his thoughts as he saw Betty walking towards him.

"Thomas, this is a nice surprise," she greeted.

He lowered his hat and beamed at her. "It's good to see you," he responded warmly. "And you too," he said to Leopold as the cat approached him. "Is this a good time?" he asked Betty.

"Yes, this is perfect. I'm almost finished organizing some files, and Elizabeth just left. Did you see her on your way in?"

Thomas nodded. "Did you have a busy day?"

"Yes, it was fairly busy," Betty answered. She gestured towards one of the round tables, indicating that Thomas should take a seat. He did, and Betty picked up a folder that she had laid on the counter. "We had a good number of customers, including the boy Ernest who I told you about," she recounted as she began organizing the papers inside of the folder.

"Yes, I remember—he's the fellow who delivered Sarah Mount's letter here," Thomas recalled brightly.

Betty nodded. "He's been coming in regularly. He likes to read all sorts of books."

"Very good," Thomas commented. "I hope he keeps up the practice of reading."

Betty smiled. "I do too. There was also some interest in our new window display."

Thomas smiled broadly. "I should hope so." He had noticed the books in the shopfront window right away. "Robert Frost is one of my favorite poets, you know."

Betty looked up to see a glimmer in his hazel eyes. There was a sparkle in her own eyes as she answered, "I didn't know that."

Thomas nodded. "Do you like his poetry?"

"I do," she responded. "He is a talented writer." She paused, and then smiled at him. "You have good taste." Before he could say anything in response, she added, "And you already know my favorite poet."

Thomas stood and crossed over to her. He remembered exactly who her favorite poet was, and it warmed his heart. "Have I told you how glad I am that you're going with me to Kansas?" he asked softly.

Betty felt a slight blush on her cheeks. "It's nice to hear that." She remained there, holding his gaze for a moment longer, and then looked down to close her folder. "That reminds me," she resumed, "I must finish packing. We leave in a week—can you believe it?"

The two of them continued chatting about their impending travel as Betty closed up the shop for the evening. They walked out together, with Leopold trotting in front of them, and felt hopeful about this adventure that they would soon embark on.

❦

Meanwhile, Bea Featherwin was at home folding laundry as she waited for Betty. She had cleaned, and hung to dry, the blouses that Betty had put into the laundry basket. She smiled as she finished the folding and walked to Betty's bedroom to place the blouses in her dresser drawer. She opened the drawer, as she recalled that Betty kept all of her folded blouses there. As she did so, she noticed that some of the clothing was rumpled. She reached inside to straighten the clothes and to make space for the clean blouses.

Her fingers suddenly brushed against the sharp corner of an envelope. Feeling curious, she pulled the envelope out. She could see that it had already been opened. She also saw that it was clearly addressed to Mr. Thomas Erwinshire, in care of the Marshfield Inn. The return address on the top listed Violet Erwinshire of Dayton, Washington as the sender. She looked at it in surprise, wondering why her daughter would have an envelope that was addressed to Thomas. She further wondered why it appeared that the envelope had already been opened.

Bea turned the envelope over, lifted the flap, and took out the letter that was folded inside. She did not mean to read the entire letter but could not stop herself once she began.

She was astonished. The letter must have been very upsetting to Thomas, she thought. She again wondered why Betty had the letter, and why Thomas may have given it to her. Whatever the case, Bea did not want Betty to know that she had found and read the letter herself. She felt increasingly uncomfortable as she continued to hold it in her hand. She replaced it in the envelope and put it back in the drawer in exactly the place she had found it. She made sure to close the drawer securely. The slight movement loosened the flap of the envelope, causing the letter to slip out a bit.

Bea placed the freshly folded clothes on the end of Betty's bed. Quietly, she stepped out and closed the door behind her. She resolved, in that moment, never to bring up the letter to anyone. It would forever be Bea's secret.

Chapter 5

Departure

The morning of the train departure arrived in the blink of an eye. The days leading up to it had been filled with work and travel preparations. Betty made sure that Elizabeth had everything she needed to manage The Sapphire Key while she and Thomas were away. This was not difficult. Elizabeth was very organized and had a good handle on the inventory and the book shipment that would be coming in. Thomas also made a couple of telephone calls to John and Charles at Erwinshire Publishing. He was able to get them up to speed on upcoming publishing deadlines and had confidence in them.

Packing luggage for the train ride, and for their stay in Kansas and Oklahoma, was not too time-consuming. Bea helped Betty choose several outfits and other essential items. The tricky part was saving space for a couple of books and paper. Betty looked forward to some time to read during the train ride, and so did Thomas. They both decided to take one small carrying case just for books, paper, and writing instruments.

With all of the packing done, Betty had extra time to spend with Bea and Leopold on the evening before her departure. Bea assured her that Leopold would be well cared-for and would receive plenty of attention. Betty had no doubt about that—Leopold was beloved by her and Bea, and by many others in town. Elizabeth had offered to stop by the house every morning to walk with the cat to The Sapphire Key. This would ensure that he continued going to the bookshop safely every day. When Betty had explained this plan to Leopold, he looked very pleased about it. With all of the love and attention he would receive, Betty felt comfortable and knew she would not need to worry about the cat.

Betty and Thomas stopped by the Highley house to speak with Mrs. Alice Highly before they left, too. They thanked her for setting everything into motion, starting with the photograph she had of her sister, Sarah, and May Bell Sebastian. She was the first one to write to Sarah and had been a huge help along the way to finding more information about Thomas' parents. She said that she was glad to help and was happy that Betty and Thomas would be able to meet and spend time with her relatives. She was even more thrilled that Thomas would finally be visiting his mother's gravesite. As a mother herself, it warmed her heart to see Thomas' interest in learning about his mother and father. She also assured Betty that Bea and Leopold were welcome to come by at any time. Betty appreciated this. She was positive that her mother would accept the open invitation. She could already imagine the two of them coming up the street to join Mrs. Highley for afternoon tea. It made her happy to know she had such good friends in town who she could rely on.

Before they left the Highleys', Clarence offered to give them a ride to the train station on the morning of their departure. It was on the way to the lumbermill, and he wanted to see them safely on their way. Betty and Thomas gladly accepted, and it was decided that he would pick them up at the Featherwins'. The plans were set, and the only thing left to do was to board the train. They would soon be on the next step of this journey to unveil the secret of Thomas' parentage.

CB

Thomas arrived at the Featherwin house early. He and Betty had time to have tea and bid farewell to Bea and Leopold before Clarence stopped by. Bea waved at them fondly as they loaded their luggage into Clarence's car, and then they went on their way.

Clarence drove into the train station with time to spare before Betty and Thomas were scheduled to board. This allowed them some time to chat. The day was cool and cloudy. A thin mist had blown in from the ocean, making the air damp. Thomas opened an umbrella once they reached the platform to shield Betty from the moisture. The two men wore coats and hats, and Betty wore a warm traveling coat.

"I hope you have a nice time," Clarence said, as they stood together. "Please say hello to Aunt Sarah and Cousin May for me."

"Of course," they replied.

"Do you have any plans while we're away?" Thomas asked.

"Father and I will stay busy at the mill," Clarence responded. "Though, I may have time on the weekend to go to the music hall. Ms. Delzell has not been there yet."

Betty gave a small smile at the mention of Ms. Inez Delzell.

"Perhaps we can all meet for lunch once Betty and I return," Thomas suggested.

"That is a fine idea," Clarence said, and Betty agreed.

Soon, it was time to board the train. Clarence checked that they had all of their luggage. They had packed light, taking one medium-sized bag and a smaller carrying case each. Satisfied that they had not left anything behind, Clarence waved and headed back to his car to drive the short distance to the lumbermill.

Standing on the train platform, luggage in hand, Betty and Thomas looked at one another in anticipation.

"We're off on our adventure," Thomas commented, and Betty smiled.

Just then, the doors to the passenger train opened. The railroad attendants offered to take their luggage and guided them inside. As they stepped onto the train, they both experienced an odd sensation. They felt that they were meant to board the train together, at that exact moment.

Ω

Betty and Thomas took some time after boarding to settle into their compartments. The train was beautifully furnished. It was just like May Mount had described to Betty when she had visited Marshfield. Each compartment contained a divan—a sofa that also functioned as a bed. There was shelving above to store luggage, and a small dresser with a mirror. Lace curtains adorned the windows, and the wood finishing gleamed throughout.

Betty was impressed at how lovely their accommodations were. This was a wonderful beginning to this important journey. She opened her luggage to place some of her items into the dresser. As she did so, she noticed a metal tin inside that she did not remember packing. She smiled happily once she took it out and opened it. The tin was filled with some of Bea's excellent berry scones, wrapped in paper. On top of the scones was a note that said, "For you and Thomas-enjoy!" Betty was touched by her mother's kind gesture and knew that she and Thomas would thoroughly enjoy the treats during their journey.

She spent the remainder of the morning reading and relaxing in her compartment. She also started to write. Betty wanted to draft an account of their journey and thought she would begin with the train ride. She had never before had a desire to write in a diary or to record her experiences. It felt important to her, however, to document this.

Just as she finished her writing for the morning, the bell in each compartment gave a little trill to announce that lunch would be served in the dining room. This was a spacious area in the center of the train, that looked and felt like a dining room one might find in a stately hotel. There were tables for two on either side of the carpeted aisle. The chairs were crafted from fine wood and had cushions on the seat and back. Kerosene lamps were available at each table in case the diners wanted extra light. It created a very welcoming and comfortable atmosphere.

Betty was pleased to find Thomas right away once she entered the dining area. He smiled at her, and the two of them sat at a table on the right side of the train. They were soon brought cups of water, as well as tea with a side of sliced lemons and sugar packets.

"This is lovely," Betty remarked.

"Yes, it is," Thomas agreed with a smile, and added a bit of sugar to his tea. "Are you settled comfortably in your compartment?"

"Yes, it's very comfortable," Betty said, and took a sip from her own cup of tea. "I did some reading and writing."

"Good. I did, too," Thomas responded.

"I organized some of my luggage also, and Mother packed a surprise," Betty continued with a smile, and showed him the metal tin that she had brought with her.

"Oh, how kind!" he exclaimed as he looked at the note and at the scones inside. They planned to enjoy one later in the afternoon.

They chatted idly for a while until the lunch arrived (soup and bread with butter), and then talked in more detail about their plans once they arrived in Kansas. Thomas' priority was to visit his mother's gravesite, though he also wanted to explore the area. He looked forward to meeting May Mount-Mosier and her family as well. He told Betty that he was still somewhat in awe about what he learned about his mother from Sarah Mount's letter. He was eager to learn as much as he could about her. Betty understood his feelings and was glad that he was so hopeful about the trip.

"I was also thinking…" Thomas said, "…about what your mother asked me at dinner: if I had told my family that we were going on this trip."

Betty nodded. Bea had asked Thomas this, and he had told her about his strained relationship with the Erwinshires. He had not seemed bothered at the dinner, and Betty was curious about what seemed to bother him now. She stirred her tea with a spoon and waited for him to continue.

"I am a bit ashamed, to be honest," he said.

This surprised Betty, and she dropped her spoon and looked at him kindly. "Oh, Thomas—"

"Not of myself," he clarified. "But I am ashamed of Aunt Violet. I do not pretend to understand her, and do not believe I ever will. I'm still just astounded that she never told me what we know now about my mother. I feel as though she has been hiding the truth from me, and to me, that is unforgivable. I truly feel that she would not be happy that I'm going on this journey. That saddens me, but it's the truth."

Betty could hear the ache of deep disappointment in his voice. Violet Erwinshire had raised him as her own child, but the love that Thomas held for her was tarnished by her recent apathy. She had shunned Thomas' questions about his parents, and Thomas did not know why. Betty, however, did have some understanding, and she could see why Violet's behavior might feel like a betrayal to him. Violet's motives had been clear in the letter that Betty had read, and that Thomas still had no knowledge of. The reminder of the letter made her uncomfortable, and she felt the color begin to drain from her face as she thought about it.

"Betty," Thomas murmured. "'Are you all right?"

She blinked and took a sip of her tea. "Yes, thank you. Your aunt's conduct towards you also saddens me. But she has no place in our journey. You were meant to know about your mother—I'm certain of that."

Thomas looked at her with such gratitude that his eyes turned a deeper shade of hazel. "Thank you for saying that."

Betty placed her hand on top of his and pressed it lightly. They both proceeded to finish their lunch, and she turned the subject to May and her daughter, Florence. She was pleased about seeing them again. She told Thomas how young Florence had taken a liking to Leopold. Thomas laughed, and remarked that he was not surprised to hear this. Leopold was a special cat, and very likeable. Betty agreed heartily and commented that the cat was likely at The Sapphire Key with Elizabeth. His routine would stay the same, Betty explained, and this would be good for him. It would be nice for Elizabeth as well, as she had grown used to him being in the bookshop.

As they talked about the bookshop, Thomas was reminded of the last time he had seen Elizabeth. She had left the shop in a hurry and had barely acknowledged him. He mentioned it to Betty. She assured him that Elizabeth had possibly been preoccupied and had meant nothing by it. Thomas accepted this explanation, and the subject was dropped.

Once they finished lunch, they walked around the train to explore their accommodations. There were several areas with upholstered chairs for lounging, and other train cars with card tables.[5] It would be a comfortable journey. Betty and Thomas agreed to meet again for dinner. Meanwhile, they would have some time to themselves to read, relax, and wash up.

As Thomas headed towards his compartment, feeling overall pleased with the journey so far, he suddenly thought of Audrey. She was the last person he dined with, before Betty, and she had recently been on a train to Washington. He was not sure why he thought of her in that moment. Perhaps it was because he had just dined with Betty in the dining car and was enjoying her company. Perhaps he felt that he should have told Betty about his dinner with Audrey.

Whatever the reason, Thomas realized that this train ride would give him and Betty time to talk and to learn more about each other. He was pleased about this, but also hesitant. He wondered if this was now the time to reveal his previous relationship or allow it to remain his secret.

---

[5] The Pullman train was manufactured by George Pullman, who designed luxury railroad cars in the 19th and 20th century. The trains were designed for "travel and sleep in safety and comfort," and its compartments (called "cars") included areas for lounging, sleeping, and dining. During the day, guests could sit in the lounge car to socialize and play cards or watch the scenery. Curtains in the sleeping compartments offered privacy, and there were separate washrooms for men and women.

Chapter 6

Luxury Living

The afternoon was spent in leisure, with reading and watching the scenery outside of the window. Thomas realized how much he needed the respite and drifted off to sleep for a while. The rest served him well, and he awoke feeling refreshed. He washed up and then had a cup of coffee delivered to his compartment. He requested that a cup be delivered to Betty, as well. The hot beverage was just what he needed to finish up his reading for work.

Betty, meanwhile, continued to make entries in her journal about their trip so far. She described the train and their lunch and was careful not to leave anything out. She did some reading also, though for pleasure and not for work. She had brought a copy of Robert Frost's poems with her and enjoyed reading through the beautiful stanzas.

At approximately three-o-clock, Thomas came to her compartment and asked if she would like to go to the lounge. He suggested that they could have tea and the berry scones that Bea had packed for them. Betty thought this was a lovely idea, and the two of them made their way to the lounge. As with the other train cars, it was decorated immaculately, with large armchairs and window seats. Lush curtains framed each window. They chose a table on the left side of the train, next to a wide window, so that they could look at the terrain outside. They were served tea, and Betty took two scones out of her metal tin. They were delicious with the tea, and even more enjoyable with a touch of the butter that the porter brought for them.[6] In the background, jazz tunes played from a Victrola.[7] The music was soft and ambient. Feeling in high spirts, they enjoyed their refreshments and commented on the view from the train window. Many birds were flying near the train tracks, and they also noticed several deer grazing along the hills. As they laughed and made small talk, Betty could not imagine an afternoon more pleasantly spent.

When the clock struck four-thirty, they left the lounge and planned to meet again for dinner later in the evening at eight-o-clock. Thomas said he would come for Betty at that time.

Once they parted, Thomas walked back in the direction of his compartment but then changed course. He stopped in an adjacent lounge and took a seat in an armchair. He thought how pleasing the day had been thus far and could not imagine a better start to this journey. There was something weighing on his mind, however. It distracted him, and he knew he must address it before much more time passed.

❧

Betty and Thomas felt as though they were walking into a party once they entered the dining room that evening. The

---

[6] Porters were part of the staff aboard the train, specifically the Pullman long-distance passenger trains. They worked as attendants, and provided various services including preparing the passengers' beds in the evening and morning; delivering room service from the dining car; sending and receiving telegrams; shining shoes; and valet service.

[7] A Victrola is a type of phonograph (an antique record player), manufactured by The Victor Talking Machine Company. It was popular throughout the early 1900s.

room was filled with guests, and it was quite a lively sight. Couples were chatting and laughing, and many were dressed in formal dining attire. The Victrola played upbeat swing music, adding to the energy in the room. Unlike earlier in the day, the curtains on each window were drawn closed and lamps at each table were lit. This gave the entire room a warm, golden glow.

Walking along the carpeted aisle, they found a table near the back of the dining car. It was fashioned like a booth, similar to those in restaurants. The seats were upholstered in material and cushioned, making them very comfortable for a leisurely dinner. In between the booth was the dining table, already set with dishware and a small vase of flowers in the center. A light fixture, suspended from the ceiling of the train, gave ample illumination. The location of the booth offered slight privacy from the rest of the diners, though they were still near enough to the main dining area. This suited them, and the comfortable booth was perfect for their first evening together.

"This has been quite a day, hasn't it?" Thomas commented, as he glanced at their surroundings.

"Yes. I was thinking, earlier, that I could not imagine a better start to our trip," Betty answered with a smile.

"I agree," he responded, and then paused to admire how lovely she looked. Her dark hair was swept up under a cloche hat[8], and she wore a navy-blue dinner dress and cream-colored gloves. The golden embroidery on the gloves brought out a hint of gold color in her eyes that Thomas could detect in the lamplight. Betty looked down to fasten a button on her glove that had come loose and did not catch

---

[8] A cloche hat is fitted, bell-shaped hat for women. It was highly popular in the 1920s.

his gaze. When she looked up again, the admiration in his eyes gave way to thoughtfulness, and he appeared as though he was about to speak.

At that moment, the waiter approached their booth to ask what they would like to drink. Thomas looked at Betty and smiled, and then said, "I'd like some hot chocolate."

Betty laughed and added, "Two of them, please."

They decided to order chicken with potatoes and vegetables. The food was delicious, and they took their time enjoying it. Thomas talked about opening his new office in Marshfield, and what he wanted it to look like. He even had an idea for the outside of the building. He was very enthusiastic, and Betty listened intently.

Betty went on to describe her vision for the coffee shop that she hoped to add on to her bookstore sometime this year. There were exciting projects in store for them, and they spent most of the evening sharing their thoughts and ideas. At the end of dinner, the waiter brought a delectable piece of cake with berries on the side. They would share this with a cup of hot tea.

It was after ten-thirty in the evening when they walked back to their individual compartments. Thomas said that he would come and get her for breakfast in the morning. Betty smiled and wished him goodnight. As she washed up and prepared to go to bed, she could not stop thinking about how perfect the evening had been.

Chapter 7

The Arrival

The train ride to Kansas had gone quicker than Betty had anticipated. The scenery was magical, and the food was better than any Betty had ever tasted. The train accommodations and service exceeded her expectations. They had truly traveled in comfort and style. Each day was better than the last, and Betty wrote every detail in her journal.

Thomas had enjoyed the journey immensely so far, and Betty could sense his enthusiasm as they neared their destination. On the day before their arrival in Pratt, Kansas, Thomas and Betty sat in the lounge looking at three photographs that Thomas brought with him. One photograph was a still portrait of a beautiful woman who was very slender and youthful. This was Thomas' mother, May Bell. The photo was not dated, but Thomas guessed that it was taken in around 1888, before May Bell had met her husband, Phillip Sebastian. The other two photographs Thomas had brought also pictured May Bell. In one, she was standing a slight distance away, and a windmill was in the background. In the other, she was holding a parasol and standing next to Sarah Mitchell Mount. This last photograph had been given to Thomas by Mrs. Alice Highley, Sarah's sister. As they looked at the photographs, they imagined what life must have been like for May Bell in Kansas. Thomas was curious about where she lived, and how she had met Sarah and Phillip. He was hopeful that he would find the answers during their stay. Betty could not help but to feel hopeful and excited too, and she could not wait to discover what lay in store for them.

The train pulled into the station in Wichita in the afternoon. Some passengers were departing the train there, while others would stay on until the train's next stop. Betty and Thomas were among the first group of passengers to disembark. The train porters assisted them with their luggage, and they soon made it onto the platform. The station was large and spacious, and quite different from the comparatively modest train depot in North Bend, Oregon. The lobby of the station building was wide and open, with a row of ticket counters. There was a large clock in the center, which chimed on the hour. Betty and Thomas walked through the lobby, in awe of the grand architecture, and made their way down the hall to the passenger waiting room. This area was also airy, with large windows that extended from floor to ceiling. There were rows of benches to accommodate the passengers waiting for their trains. The room had a good view of the outside, and Betty and Thomas could see several Model-T cars driving up to the curb.[9]

They waited in the comfortable room and looked out the window. Soon, another Model-T drove up, and a woman and girl stepped out. Betty quickly recognized them.

"That's May and Florence," she told Thomas happily.

"Excellent," he responded with a smile. He caught the attention of a station attendant, who came to assist Betty with her luggage. They all walked out and met May Mount-Mosier and her daughter, Florence. May smiled at Betty, and Florence skipped up to her to greet her with a hug.

"It's so good to see you," Betty said to the young girl, and then introduced Thomas to her.

---

[9] Wichita, Kansas was a booming, industrialized city in the 1920s and 1930s. It was home to the Union Station (train station), large hospitals, and many other businesses.

"Hello, it's nice to meet you," Thomas greeted. Florence nodded, and then May joined them. Introductions between May and Thomas were made, and then the four of them climbed into the car to begin the drive to the Mosier house in Pratt.

They chatted for the duration of the drive. Betty and Thomas recounted the train journey, and May told them about the town of Pratt and its proximity to Oklahoma. Travel between the two states, Kansas and Oklahoma, was common and easily managed by car or carriage. The drive from Pratt, Kansas to Gate, Oklahoma was not long, and May liked the convenience of being near her mother, Sarah. Her mother was looking forward to receiving them in several days and was particularly glad about meeting Thomas. May and her husband, Lester, were thrilled to have Betty and Thomas as their guests for these next couple of days. May explained that Lester worked as a pharmacist in town and stayed quite busy. May worked as a nurse at the local hospital four days per week, and Florence was in grade school. Florence had begged May to let her go to the train station to pick up Betty and Thomas. May allowed this and had fetched her daughter from school early.

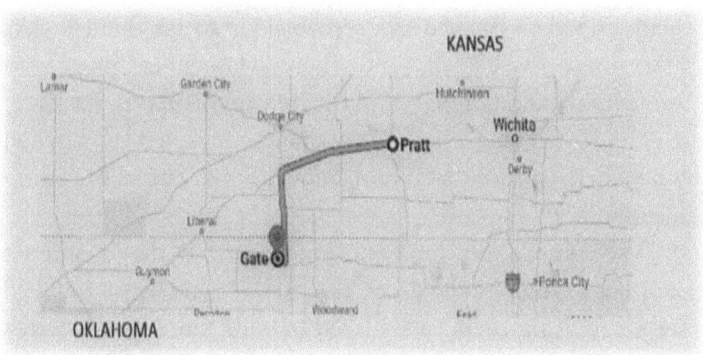

Betty and Thomas were enjoying the conversation so much that the time seemed to fly by. They were surprised when they reached a cream-colored house with bay windows and a front porch. Betty noticed that it was similar in style and design to her home in Marshfield. May pulled the car up to the house, and announced, "We're home."

Florence stepped out of the car first and startled a rooster that had been resting on the porch. The land surrounding the house was flat and unpaved. Several barren trees stood around the perimeter, and small birds flew back and forth between them. The neighboring houses were a good distance away. From her vantage point, Betty could see more flat land with a spattering of trees, and a horse stable just down the road. A couple of dogs were chasing each other. It was a rural area, and quite different from what Betty and Thomas were accustomed to.

As Betty stepped out of the car and breathed in the air, she felt a tingle of anticipation and adventure. She looked at Thomas and was sure that he was feeling the same way. He smiled at her and took her bag so that she would only need to hold her small carrying case. May offered to take Thomas' carrying case in. He thanked her, and they stepped onto the porch. Florence was sitting on a rocking chair, waiting for them, and then opened the screen door to let them inside. The house was cool, and there was something very comfortable and familiar about it that immediately set Betty at ease. It had two levels. Downstairs contained the kitchen and main living area. Betty presumed that the bedrooms were upstairs.

"Welcome," May said, and gestured that they could set their bags down by the door. They did so, and again thanked her for inviting them to stay. "Not at all," she replied, with a wave of her hand, and insisted that they take a seat in the kitchen and relax. She poured them each a glass of iced tea. Florence took one sip, and then asked if she could play outside. "Yes, but stay close to the house," May said.

With a triumphant smile, Florence said, "See you later!" to Betty and Thomas before leaving out the back door.

May smiled and shook her head fondly, and then joined Betty and Thomas at the table. "That girl has more energy than I know what to do with sometimes," she commented, and Betty laughed. "The bedrooms are upstairs. You each have your own room," she continued.

"That's perfect," Betty replied. She realized what was so familiar about the house. It reminded her a bit of Mrs. Highley's house, especially the kitchen. There was also a likeness between Mrs. Highley and May that Betty had not noticed before. It was something in May's voice and gestures, and it made Betty feel glad. Unbeknownst to Betty, Thomas had noticed the likeness too, and it made him feel like he was home.

May took a sip from her glass, and then glanced at the clock on the wall. "Lester will be home shortly. He'll be pleased to meet you. In the meantime, I can show you to your rooms."

Betty and Thomas agreed, and followed her up the stairs with their bags. There were two bedrooms on either end of the hall. The two guestrooms were next to one another on one end. Betty chose to stay in the room at the very end of the hall. Thomas, of course, would stay in the room to her right. May returned downstairs to allow them some time to settle in and said she would let them know when her husband had arrived.

The rooms were neatly furnished and comfortable. Betty set her bags near the end of the bed and lifted out a couple of her blouses that lay folded inside to shake out the creases.

She then sat in the rocking chair near the window in the room, and simply thought about how exciting it was to finally be in Kansas. She wondered how Thomas was feeling. He was in the town where his mother had lived, and they would soon be visiting her gravesite. She could only imagine what emotions he was experiencing. She felt amazed that all of their discoveries had led them to this point. This was a significant step for Thomas and would likely be an emotional journey for him. Betty would support him through everything.

She freshened up in the adjacent washroom, and when she stepped out, Thomas was at the head of the staircase. He beamed at her, and said that May's husband, Lester, had just arrived home. She took his arm as he extended it to her, and they walked down the stairs and back into the kitchen. A tall man, in a gray suit and tie, stood by the front door, placing his hat on the hat rack. May was in the kitchen, stirring a pot of soup, and Florence had returned inside and sat at the table. She had washed up for dinner, and had changed clothes too, likely at her mother's insistence.

"Oh, there you are," May exclaimed as she noticed Betty and Thomas entering. "Lester, dear, please meet our guests."

The tall man turned around and approached them. He had very kind eyes and a warm smile. "Hello," he greeted, and reached to shake Thomas' hand. "I'm Lester Mosier, May's husband. You must be Thomas."

"Yes, sir," Thomas replied. "It's good to meet you."

He smiled again and murmured, "Call me Lester." He turned to Betty and briefly took her hand. "Ms. Betty Featherwin. May and Florence have told me about you, and your cat."

Betty grinned. "I'm so glad to meet you. It's a pleasure to be here with all of you."

Thomas nodded, wholeheartedly agreeing with this statement. After exchanging some small talk about their day, the five of them sat down to dinner and became better acquainted. Betty told the Mosiers about The Sapphire Key, and how she often visited with the Highleys. May knew that Betty and Bea Featherwin were close friends of her aunt. She was pleased to hear that Mrs. Highley, her husband, and her son, Clarence, were doing well. Thomas told them about his business, Erwinshire Publishing, and his plan to open a second office in Marshfield. May knew about Thomas' quest to find more information about his mother and was happy to get to know him better. She had never known May Bell Sebastian, but her mother, Sarah, had been good friends with her.

The conversation turned to Betty and Thomas' plans for their time in Kansas.

"One of the first things I'd like to do..." Thomas said, "...is to visit my mother's gravesite."

Betty could hear his voice soften, and she unconsciously brushed her hand against his. He noticed the gesture and squeezed her hand in return.

May nodded. "Of course. It is located at Greenlawn Cemetery, which is fairly close by.[10] When would you like to go?"

Thomas glanced briefly at Betty, asking her an unspoken question, and she nodded. He replied, "Tomorrow, if that is possible."

"Yes, that is not a problem. You can borrow the car to drive there. It's just a couple of miles from here."

"Thank you," Thomas said. "That's very kind."

---

[10] Greenlawn Cemetery was established in Pratt, Kansas in 1885. It spans 35 acres.

May went on to explain the best route to the cemetery. Lester commented that they would do better with a map. He pulled a folded map out of his vest pocket and handed it to Thomas.

They continued to talk casually for a little while. Florence asked about Leopold, and Betty told her that he was doing well and had enjoyed playing with her when she came to visit. Florence asked if the cat still worked at Betty's bookshop. Betty laughed in response and told her, "Yes, and he does a very good job." Florence was glad about that, but still wanted her own cat. Her parents had not given her permission yet. Thomas looked at Betty quizzically after dinner, wondering what Florence had meant about Leopold working at the bookshop. Betty smiled and let him in on the story that Leopold's job was to greet customers. Thomas found this clever, and also somewhat true.

By eight-o-clock, dinner was over, and May had the task of getting her daughter ready for bed. Thomas and Betty both felt a little tired after their long day and excused themselves to retire for the evening. The Mosiers wished them a good night's sleep, and May promised to leave the car and keys out for them in the morning.

As they ascended the staircase, Thomas whispered to Betty, "I'm so glad that we're finally here. And I'm glad that you're here with me."

Betty looked over at him, noticing the warmth in his eyes, and nodded. "I'm glad too, and so happy for you."

Thomas could hear the sincerity in her voice and knew that she was just as happy to be in Kansas as he was. She had given him unwavering support, and he could see how much she had enjoyed the trip so far. He realized how much he would appreciate her continued support, especially during the visit to the cemetery tomorrow. He had given the visit a lot of thought and decided that he did not want to go alone. He hoped that Betty would feel comfortable with accompanying him.

Betty seemed to know what he was thinking. When they reached the top of the stairs, she said, "Would you like me to go with you tomorrow to the cemetery?"

Thomas nodded. "Yes, I really would."

Betty gave him a soft smile. "I'm happy to come and would like to bring some flowers for the gravesite."

Thomas sighed, "Thank you," and knew, in that moment, that there was no other person in the world he would rather be with on this journey.

They would visit the gravesite tomorrow, and from there they only wondered what they might uncover. As they retired to their separate rooms, they found it hard to fall asleep. When sleep eventually came, it was riddled with fragmented images of the woman who had brought them to the Midwest.

Chapter 8

The Visit

The next morning, Thomas and Betty awoke to the smell of coffee and bacon. They washed up and made their way downstairs and into the kitchen. Lester had already left for work, and Florence was still sleeping. May had prepared a platter of scrambled eggs, fresh biscuits, jam, and bacon.

Thomas commented to Betty, "That smells so good; I didn't realize how hungry I was."

Just then, May Mosier entered the kitchen. "Please sit," she said in greeting. "I'll get you some coffee." Betty and Thomas thanked her. "You are very welcome," May replied. "I cook a good breakfast every morning."

As they ate breakfast and drank their coffee, the three of them discussed the drive to the cemetery. Thomas had the map that Lester had given to him, which would be very helpful. Betty mentioned that she would like to take flowers to the cemetery.

May smiled at this. "After breakfast, we can go out back and cut some flowers from my flower garden. I have ribbon to wrap around them." Betty thought this was a wonderful idea. May agreed, and then glanced over at Thomas and added, "This is an important day."

So far, this journey had gone exactly the way Thomas had imagined. He felt so grateful that he could visit his mother's gravesite, and perhaps view where the accident happened so many years ago. He hoped to stop by the sheriff's office to get more information on the exact location, if they even had any information, as it had been such a long time ago. May assured them that she did not need the car, so Betty and Thomas could go on ahead and take their time. They thanked her again and said they would see her at dinner.

Thomas sat behind the wheel, and Betty kept the map in her hand to guide them. The small bouquet of purple and white flowers she had selected from May's garden rested on her lap. As they drove away, she noticed that Florence was on the front porch with her dog, waving goodbye. Betty gave a quick wave, and they were on their way.

ભ

In less than a half-hour, they arrived at an intersection in the road. After checking the map, Thomas drove a bit further until he reached a brick structure with a metal sign attached to it that read, in large capital letters, "Greenlawn Cemetery."

Thomas let out an audible breath. "This is it."

Betty looked over at him and saw his fingers drumming against the steering wheel. He had stopped the car to read the sign.

"Thomas," Betty muttered softly. Her voice seemed to revive him, and he continued driving forward past the sign and onto the cemetery grounds. The landscape was flat and mostly bare, with few patches of grass. As they moved slowly down the road to reach an area to park the car, Betty noticed the various headstones on the ground. She felt a sense of reverence as they drove past. This was a sacred place.

They came upon an area where other cars were parked. A car was just ahead of them, pulling into the open area. Thomas followed suit and parked right behind. As Betty looked around, she could see other people on the cemetery grounds. Some knelt beside headstones, while others were content to walk. It reminded her, for a fleeting moment, of the cemetery in Marshfield. When she would visit the cemetery with her mother, sometimes they sat at her father's headstone. On other occasions, they had simply walked the grounds. Bea had once said that a loved one's spirit could be felt everywhere, not just at the gravesite. Betty gradually believed that this was true.

She cleared her mind of her father and returned her attention to Thomas. He had parked, and now sat quietly gazing out at the grounds just as Betty had been doing. Visiting her own father's grave had been difficult, and she imagined that this experience would be even more difficult for Thomas. Unlike Betty, Thomas was never granted the opportunity to mourn his parent. As he continued to sit in the car, Betty could understand his hesitancy and the myriad of emotions that he was likely experiencing. This was a momentous occasion for him, and she wanted him to experience it on his own terms.

After a few moments, Thomas looked over at her with a mixture of determination and sadness in his eyes. He opened the door, stepped out of the car, and then walked around to open Betty's door for her. Without saying a word, he offered his hand. She placed her hand in his and they walked slowly to the area of dirt and grass where the assortment of headstones began.

"I'm ready," Thomas uttered softly. Betty nodded, and they continued walking and passing headstones. It was a quiet morning, and the air was cool and breezy. The sun streamed delicately through the clouds, casting rays of light onto the ground. They did not know where May Bell Sebastian's headstone would be, but they continued on and trusted that they would find it. Lester had mentioned that older headstones would be at the far left of the cemetery.

After a stretch of time walking and breathing in the morning air, they paused at a spot that was surrounded by a circle of trees and a sprinkling of flowering dogwood, the small white flower native to Kansas. It was a beautiful spot. As they drew near, sunlight streamed down to shine upon one of the headstones. Betty and Thomas glanced at one another, and then, hand in hand, walked closer.

A grey, rectangular headstone lay embedded into the ground and encircled with the flowing dogwood. A name was carved into the stone, in distinct capital letters, followed by dates. The headstone read, "May Bell Sebastian. 1872-1897." There was a carving of a small, five-pointed star on the headstone between the dates.

Betty felt Thomas falter just as she heard his sharp intake of breath. She placed her other hand on his arm to steady him, and he entwined his fingers with hers. Betty could sense the emotions coursing within him—not just grief but regret and longing. As she stood with him, gazing upon the beautiful spot where his mother's headstone lay, Betty's own heart ached. It ached for Thomas now, and for May Bell. Most of all, it ached for the boy who had never known his mother. Betty felt her eyes begin to blur as she looked at the dates etched on the headstone. 1872-1897. May Bell had been just twenty-five years old when she had died. She had left this world far too soon, and there was no justification for it.

Betty could feel Thomas' hand loosen from hers. She blinked and saw him bend down to kneel at the headstone. She remembered that she had the bouquet of flowers tucked under her arm, and she joined him in kneeling. May Mosier had thoughtfully tied a purple ribbon around the stems. Betty placed her hand gently on Thomas' shoulder.

When he looked up, he smiled at her. There was dampness on his cheek, but the expression in his eyes had changed. The sadness remained, but with it was a sense of having found peace. Betty placed the bouquet near the top of the headstone, and the effect was beautiful. The small, pale purple flowers mixed with the white ones complimented the dogwood. It made a wreath, or halo, around "May Bell Sebastian." As they stood up, continuing to gaze at her gravesite, they felt that the world had shifted and realigned to make sense of things that did not make sense before. They had been led to this spot and were meant to be there to honor the memory of Thomas' mother.

At length, Thomas spoke. His voice sounded strong within the quiet and stillness of their surroundings. "I'm very glad that we came," he said. "I feel more…" he paused, as if trying to find the right words. "I feel more complete, and more at peace, now that I know where she is buried."

Betty nodded and could understand his feelings. It had taken him so long, and so many years, to learn the truth about his mother. It took him longer still to arrive here, at this place and in this moment, where he could begin to process her death.

"I think coming here was important," Betty responded. She turned to look at him. "I'm glad that it has allowed you to find some peace."

Thomas nodded. "Thank you for being here. Thank you for everything."

Betty merely shook her head softly. They walked back towards the car, unhurried in their steps. Before they reached it, they stopped to stand in a patch of sunlight. The breeze was picking up, and it moved gently through the trees. It would be a lovely day. The people starting to trickle in had a temperate afternoon to look forward to.

Time had seemed to stand still in the tranquil atmosphere of the cemetery. Thomas glanced at his pocket watch and was startled to see it was already mid-morning. They took their remaining steps towards the car, and only then Betty realized that Thomas had been holding her hand during the entire walk back. He released it to open the car door, and they climbed inside.

As they drove back towards the entrance, and the "Greenlawn Cemetery" sign they had passed on the way, they remained silent. Thomas turned the corner and spotted a café. He asked Betty if she would mind stopping in.

They would plan the rest of their day, and the rest of their trip. But first, they would sit in the café with a hot cup of coffee to chat and reflect on what had happened so far.

Chapter 9

Pratt Café

The sign on the café door read, "Pratt Café" in pine-green letters. It had the look of a building that had stood for many years. Thomas opened the door for Betty, and then walked in after her. The café had an atmosphere of warmth, and of home, just like the Mosier house. There were wooden booths throughout, and a long counter lined with plates and mugs. The scent of coffee and eggs lingered in the air, and the sounds of cooking were coming from the kitchen behind the counter. There were other people sitting throughout the café, some in booths and other at round tables. A waitress was bustling around to get everyone's order.

They took a seat at a booth just to the right of the door. It was pleasant to sit in the warm environment of the café, and they did not mind the brief pause before the waitress came by their table. It gave them time to think and chat. When they had found May Bell's headstone, Betty had immediately noticed the five-pointed star emblem etched in between her birth and death dates. She had continued to think about it during the drive to the café. As she sat down in the booth, across from Thomas, she suddenly knew why the emblem had caught her attention. She had seen it before.

"Thomas," she said, "Did you notice the star emblem on your mother's headstone?"

He nodded and looked at her curiously. "Yes, I did. I was so deep in thought while we were there, that I almost forgot about seeing that symbol. I recognized it, but I can't place where I may have seen it before."

Betty smiled. "I recognized it as well. I saw it on headstones in the cemetery where my father is buried in Marshfield. It is the symbol for a charitable organization called the Order of the Eastern Star."[11]

Thomas' eyes widened. "Yes, that sounds familiar."

"My mother told me that it is an important organization that many women are involved in. I also remember Mrs. Highley saying that many of the Mount women are members. They support the community through charitable work and public service."

Thomas nodded, recognition flickering in his eyes.

"Clearly, your mother was a member," Betty continued. "This is another piece of information that we have discovered about her."

"Yes, indeed," Thomas breathed, and leant back. A faraway expression crossed his face as he considered this new information. He could almost see his mother as a young woman, bustling about town to visit her good friend, Sarah Mitchell Mount, and meeting with other women in the Order of the Eastern Star. He was about to share his thoughts with Betty, when the waitress arrived at their booth.

"Hello there, and thank you for waiting," the waitress greeted. She looked like a kind woman, with bright eyes and a wide smile. She had the demeanor of someone who had worked in the café for a long time and was knowledgeable

---

[11] The Order of the Eastern Star (OES) is a fraternal organization that still exists today. Membership is open to men and women and is based on relationships. Men must be Master Masons and women must have specific familial relationships with Masons. Members partake in community service and other charitable projects to support community needs.

in the history of the café and the surrounding town. "Would you like some coffee?"

"Yes, please," Betty answered, and smiled at the woman.

"You've got it," she replied. She turned towards the counter, poured coffee from a pot into two cups, and then brought the steaming cups to them.

"Thank you," Thomas said.

"Of course," she replied. "Any breakfast for you two?"

"No, thank you," they replied. The waitress nodded and walked over to attend to customers at another table.

Betty and Thomas began to sip their coffee, and Thomas shared his thoughts about his mother and what life may have been like for her. He was curious to learn more and wanted more details about the carriage accident that caused her death. Betty was interested in the carriage accident too and agreed that this would be the next phase of their journey.

Just as they were discussing this, the waitress came up to their booth again. She brought a piece of berry pie on a plate, and two forks.

"I know you didn't order this," she said with a smile, as they looked at her. "But I made this pie this morning. I would like your opinion on it." They smiled in response, and quickly took a bite.

"Oh, this pie is wonderful," Betty murmured as she tasted the rich, sweet raspberries and blueberries.

"It's very good," Thomas agreed.

The waitress grinned. "I don't bake many pies, so I'm glad you like it," she said. "My name is Nora. I've lived here for thirty years with my husband, and we run this café together."

"Oh, you must know this town well," Betty replied.

She nodded, and then looked at Thomas and studied his face, as if trying to place him. "Are you from around here?" she asked.

Thomas shook his head. "No, we're just visitors."

Nora smiled softly, and replied, "You look a little familiar to me."

Thomas grinned in response, and he thought to himself that perhaps this waitress had known his mother. As Nora placed napkins on the table for them, he realized that this theory might not be so far-fetched.

He looked at her and asked, "Do you remember a carriage accident that happened about twenty years ago in this area? From what I understand, the carriage rolled down a ravine and stopped near a creek."

Nora nodded emphatically. "I sure do. Many folks around here remember the accident. Phillip Sebastian and his wife were in that carriage. He used to come in here often." She paused, and then her voice softened as she added, "It was a real tragedy. Luckily, their baby was left with friends or else he would have died in that accident too." Her eyes drifted towards the window for a moment as she reflected. "I don't know what happened to the baby. We were all devastated that he lost both of his parents."

Thomas looked at her with great sadness is his eyes. He said softly, "I am that baby. My name is Thomas, and my parents were Phillip and May Sebastian."

Nora's jaw dropped in astonishment. She looked at his face with renewed recognition in her eyes, and then said, "Please, come with me now."

They followed her to the middle of the café, to a wall that was covered in framed photos. Nora scanned the wall briefly, and then pointed to a photograph of a man and woman seated together. The woman was holding a baby in her lap.

"That is you, with your parents," Nora said to Thomas, with a note of astonishment in her voice. "Your mother gave me that photo."

Betty's eyes widened in amazement. Thomas felt his voice crack, but he could not say anything. He was overwhelmed and filled with such elation. It was hard to believe that he was looking at photo of his parents. A photo of his family.

Nora placed her hand on Thomas' arm. "I will have my husband take it down. This photo belongs to you."

Thomas was at a loss for words, and merely nodded. He walked back towards the booth, and Betty followed him. She too was speechless.

In a few moments, an older man approached. He placed the photograph on the table, and said, with a bow of his head, "I'm sorry about your parents," and then walked away to leave them to their thoughts.

Betty and Thomas managed to drink their coffee, though remained silent and absorbed in their thoughts. To have met someone who knew Phillip Sebastian, and then to have this photograph, was incredible. They both felt that someone was guiding them on this journey.

Thomas stared at the photo, wanting to study every detail. Betty could sense that he was deeply affected and trying to process everything he had learned.

Nora returned shortly and smiled with a motherly kindness at Thomas. "No charge," she said. "I'm so pleased to meet the son of Phillip and May."

Thomas found his voice and asked, "Do you know exactly where the accident occurred?"

"Oh, it's about an hour down the road," she replied. "There's a sign labeled, 'Creek Road.' You'll see a fork in the road and a ravine. That's where the carriage overturned. A few homes have been built around there since the accident."

Thomas looked over at Betty. She knew what he was thinking. He wished to visit that spot. They would be headed there next.

They thanked Nora and said how fortunate it was that they decided to stop by the café for coffee. Nora agreed, and gave Thomas a hug in parting. Thomas told her that he and Betty lived in Marshfield, Oregon, and that he was planning to open an office for his publishing business there. She was glad to hear this and said she would love to hear more about it. She gave him a café menu and asked that he keep in touch.

"Write to me," she requested. "The menu has our address on it."

Thomas smiled. "I will certainly do that."

They said a final goodbye, and exited the café feeling lighter than when they had first entered. Thomas held the photograph in his hands protectively, looking at it again as they walked towards the car. He paused as they reached the car and looked at Betty.

"This has been amazing, Thomas," she said softly. "Just amazing."

"Yes, it has," he responded, with a renewed energy in his voice. "I'm ready to continue and see where this journey leads us."

Betty smiled. "Me too."

He approached to open the car door for her and looked at her with deep appreciation in his hazel eyes. They climbed into the car and were soon headed in the direction of the area Nora had described as "Creek Road." They were both eager to see the location of the carriage accident and wondered what else they might discover on the way.

Chapter 10

Creek Road

It took Thomas and Betty a little over an hour to find Creek Road. The terrain was rugged with a deep ravine, and parts of the land appeared to be eroded from years of wind and rain. The surrounding area had hills and slopes, and down below at the bottom of the ravine was a bubbling creek. There were indentations and small, cavernous openings at the base of the ravine, as well. As they parked and exited the car to look at the landscape, Betty imagined how treacherous it might be for a carriage traveling through. If it was dark or rainy, the wheels of a carriage could easily twist or become lodged in the earth. For a moment, Betty could see the accident before her eyes. She could hear the shriek of the horses, and the deafening shatter as the carriage collapsed down into the creek.

She shuddered, and felt Thomas stand near her and place his hand on her arm. "This is where it happened," he said slowly. "It's a scenic area, but I can also see how it could be dangerous."

Betty nodded. "I wonder if there are reports of the accident. Surely, the papers would have printed the story at the time."

"Yes, there must be reports," Thomas replied, and placed his hand at her elbow to steady her as they walked across the uneven terrain. They stopped a short distance away from the ravine for safety, though maintained a good vantage point to see the creek and caverns below. "The sheriff's office would likely have the information."

"I agree," Betty responded. They took one more look at the creek and grassy hills. She wondered if there had been any chance that May Bell and Phillip could have been saved. Looking at the creek, and the drastic drop from where they stood to the bottom of the ravine, she felt sad, and like she already knew the answer. There was one way to find out for sure.

"Shall we go on to the sheriff's office?" she asked, starting to pull Lester's map out of her coat pocket.

"Yes," Thomas answered, and they turned away to head back to the car. "Did you find it on the map?"

Betty nodded and indicated a spot about five miles down the road. Thomas looked to see which direction he would need to travel, and then the two of them climbed back into the car to continue to the next stop in their journey.

ভ

The sheriff's office was a large building along a street that was barren, except for a drug store next door. The outside of the office and surrounding area were quiet and peaceful. The sun had broken through the clouds, though the temperature remained cool and there was a slight breeze. The atmosphere was so still and dormant that Betty and Thomas expected to find the inside of the sheriff's office just as subdued.

They entered and were greeted with the exact opposite of what they had expected. The sheriff's office was full of activity. People were bustling around, walking from one end of the office to the other with papers in their hands. Men in uniform—the sheriff's deputies—spoke in loud voices over a group of people that were clustered along the side wall. Four children, who looked to be eight or nine years old, stood and talked over one another. One of the children, a young girl, appeared to be crying. Adults, presumably the children's parents, stood around them. They were talking to a police officer, who was trying to hear over all of the commotion. The sound of ringing telephones added to the noise in the room.

Betty and Thomas glanced at one another, wondering if they had arrived at the wrong time. Just then, a man wearing a heavy jacket and a hat with a silver badge on the rim approached them. The badge on his hat said, "Pratt County Sheriff's Department." He also wore a badge on his jacket, which said, "Sheriff."

"Good afternoon," he greeted them quickly. "It's a busy day here for us. How can I help you folks?"

Thomas shook his hand. "Thank you, Sherriff. We can see how busy you are, and we don't want to take too much of your time."

"It's all right," the sheriff responded, and glanced over at the group of children and their parents. "My deputies are handling it. We don't usually have this much excitement, but when a body is found, the news travels fast and the whole town is over here in a matter of minutes."

Thomas and Betty looked at him with wide eyes. "A body was found?" Thomas repeated in surprise.

"Yes," the sheriff answered, and rubbed his whiskered chin with his hand. "Some kids were playing near a creek about five miles down the road. There are some caves down at the bottom of a ravine, and they went inside to play or hide," he explained. "Turns out that there is a body in one of the caves. One of the children stumbled upon it several hours ago, and then the whole group—" he gestured to the children and adults— "came by to report it." He frowned, and continued, "It was quite upsetting to that little girl, of course. A long-deceased body is a startling thing to find, even for an adult."

Betty and Thomas looked at the sheriff, dumbfounded. The creek and ravine he had described sounded just like the area they had just visited.

"Sheriff," Betty said slowly, "Are you talking about the area called Creek Road?"

"Yes, that's where the children found the body."

Betty nearly gasped. Thomas, too, looked shocked, but then his expression changed. "How long has the body been there?" he asked.

"It's hard to tell for sure. A coroner is at the scene now. He can tell us more after he completes the investigation, and hopefully identify the body. But it is mostly bones and looks like the remains of someone who has been there for quite some time." He paused, and then looked at Thomas and continued, "You seem interested in this, but that's not the reason you came in. Did you have something to report?"

"Actually," Thomas replied, lowering his voice slightly, "I wanted to ask about a carriage accident that happened by Creek Road, some twenty years ago."

Betty drew in a breath. She knew where Thomas was headed. Sarah Mitchell Mount had said in her letter to Thomas that all of the people in the carriage had been killed. This included the driver, May Bell, and Phillip. The driver and May Bell had been identified, but Phillip's body had never been recovered. She had also said that there were rumors that Phillip had been seen walking around Seattle, Washington in the year after the accident. Sarah had never believed these rumors. Thomas did not believe them either. After reading Sarah's letter, he had told Betty that he was sure his father had died in the accident, and he was determined to find out what had truly happened.

Betty held her breath in anticipation as Thomas continued. "Three people were killed in the accident. Two of the bodies were found and identified, but one was not. Is it possible that the remains in the cave belong to that third person killed in the carriage accident? The name is Phillip Sebastian."

The sheriff looked at Thomas with a puzzled expression on his face. "I'm very familiar with that carriage accident," he said. "Everyone was listed as dead. From our accounts, Phillip Sebastian was declared dead as well. But you're correct—we never identified his body." The sheriff frowned then and looked sternly at Thomas. "What is your interest in this?"

Thomas straightened, looked the sheriff in the eye, and said, "My name is Thomas Sebastian. I am the son of May Bell and Phillip Sebastian."

He said the words with such conviction that the sheriff grew silent for a moment. He cleared his throat, and said to Thomas, "You can stay, but it will take a couple of hours to gather the remains and for the coroner to generate a report."

Thomas nodded, and in a firm voice, replied, "Thank you."

The sheriff then left them to return to the group that was speaking with a police officer. Betty was in utter disbelief and lost for words as Thomas offered his arm to her. They looked for somewhere to sit, but the office was so crowded that they decided to go next door to the drug store instead. They walked out to the covered porch of the drug store which had tables and chairs. It was a comfortable, breezy spot, and would be suitable as they waited for the results of the coroner's investigation.

As Betty reached for a chair at one of the tables, she felt a sudden wave of exhaustion and nearly collapsed into it. Thomas felt exhausted too, but also exhilarated. He pulled the chair out for her and held her arm for a moment before she sat down. He studied her face, and gently tucked a strand of her hair behind her ear that had fallen loose in the breeze.

"Thomas," she murmured at his touch.

"Are you all right?" he asked softly.

She gave a slight nod. "Are you?"

He closed his eyes and breathed in. "Yes." He opened his eyes to look at her, and continued, "I've been waiting twenty-three years for this."

Betty could only guess at what was going through his mind. He had such strength of spirit, and such determination. It was amazing to see his perseverance and his loyalty to his mother and father. "You have waited a long time," Betty responded. "And we've had so many discoveries, just today." She sank into the chair, and Thomas sat down in a chair across from her. "Are you ready for this?" she asked.

He nodded. "I didn't think I would be ready, but now I must know the entire truth." He looked contemplative, and continued, "This all started when you were speaking with Mrs. Highley and May Mosier last year. If you had not been at that gathering, and had not had that conversation, we might not be here today."

He referred to the conversation Betty had with the two women about the story of a carriage accident and a boy named "Thomas E.". The connection between the story and Thomas had been unknown at the time. Thomas was correct. If Betty had not been there, and had not been part of that conversation, they may never have uncovered the truth about Thomas' parents. The thought sent a chill through her.

Thomas took the photograph from the café out of his large coat pocket. He looked at it for a moment, and then, with a slight crack in his voice, he said, "This is my family."

Betty placed her hand over his. "It is a beautiful photo," she said softly. "You are a Sebastian."

These words fortified him. For the first time in his life, he had a solid sense of his identity and where he had come from. He continued to look at the photograph of his mother and father. His mother had held him in her arms. She had been alive, and a part of this community twenty-three years ago, along with his father. He glanced back at Betty and was suddenly filled with an undeniable realization.

He had found his family.

Chapter 11

The Sheriff's Office

They passed the time on the drug store porch. Thomas went inside after an hour-and-a-half had passed and came back out with two drinks from the soda fountain and wrapped chicken sandwiches. They both were glad to have the refreshment of the soda but found themselves too anxious to eat. Thomas wondered how the coroner's investigation was progressing, and whether any items would be found among the remains. Mostly, he wondered if his suspicion was correct that the remains belonged to Phillip Sebastian. Betty wondered also.

Their patience was soon rewarded, and they saw the coroner's vehicle pull into the parking area. A man exited the vehicle and entered the sheriff's office. Betty and Thomas looked at one another, and then rose to their feet to follow the man inside. They could see the coroner speaking to the sheriff, and he appeared to hand him something. The sheriff noticed Betty and Thomas standing by the door and motioned for them to come over.

"The coroner believes that the bones are very old," the sheriff explained. "Perhaps twenty years old." He held something wrapped in a cloth in hands. He pulled back the corners of the cloth to reveal a round, silver object. "This pocket watch was found among the remains."

He carefully handed the cloth and pocket watch to Thomas to inspect. Thomas studied the watch with intrigue. The face of the watch was cracked and disintegrated, but the back was intact. He used the cloth to gently clean away some dirt. As he did so, the silver color of the watch became more prominent, and he revealed initials engraved into the backing. The initials, in slanted script, were "*P.S.*"

Thomas knew in an instant that the watch belonged to his father. "These initials, P.S., stand for Phillip Sebastian," he said, and looked up at the sheriff and coroner. "This must be my father's watch."

The sheriff nodded, and the coroner made a note on his writing board. "We believe that the carriage rolled down the hill so fast that your father was thrown out and into a cave. He was so hidden that no one was able to locate his body. It was a terrible accident, and there were no survivors. As you may know, the bodies of May Bell Sebastian and the driver were found in the creek."

This was the first time Thomas had heard where his mother's body had been found. He had, in the back of his mind, prepared for this information, but hearing it spoken aloud pained him in a way he had not anticipated. Betty noticed the shudder that passed across his face as the sheriff spoke, and she slipped her hand in his. He squeezed it in return.

The sheriff had also noticed Thomas' reaction to hearing where May Bell had been found and paused for a moment with a kind look on his face. He then asked if Thomas would mind filling out some paperwork, stating his relationship to the deceased and his knowledge of the accident. Thomas said he was happy to do so. He also said that he would like to keep the pocket watch. The sheriff and coroner found no issue with this and were glad to turn the watch over to Thomas. The watch rightfully belonged to him, as Phillip Sebastian's next-of-kin.

Thomas took a seat in the office to complete the paperwork while the sheriff and coroner finished writing up their report. He wrote what he knew about the accident and indicated that he was the only child of Phillip and May Sebastian. He also indicated that he had been raised by May's sister, Violet, after the death of his parents. Betty sat with him quietly as he did this.

The sheriff returned shortly with a copy of the coroner's report and Thomas thanked him. "Before you leave," the sheriff said, "you should know that the local newspaper plans to print a story about this."

"Oh," Thomas and Betty responded in unison. This was not surprising to hear, as this was a significant story for Pratt County.

"They would like to include a photograph of you, holding your father's pocket watch," the sheriff continued. "Is that all right with you?"

Thomas was honored by this. The truth about what had happened to his father would finally come to light, and it had been a long time coming. He told the sheriff that he would gladly stand for a photograph, and then followed him to a room near the back of the office. A newspaper reporter and a photographer were there to greet him. Betty remained in the main part of the office to wait for him.

When Thomas and the sheriff came out of the room after a few minutes, Betty was pleased to see that Thomas had a smile on his face. He was thanking the sheriff.

"I should thank you, as well," the sheriff replied. "You finally closed this case for us. Are you and your wife staying in town for a while?"

Betty blushed slightly at the misinterpretation of herself and Thomas, but she did not correct the sheriff, as it seemed impolite to do so. Neither did Thomas. He swiftly answered that they were staying with Lester and May Mosier in Pratt for a couple of days, before returning to Oregon at the end of the week. He then told the sheriff that he had visited his mother's gravesite at Greenlawn Cemetery and felt it appropriate that his father be buried next to her.

The sheriff looked solemn and called the coroner over. The coroner listened to Thomas' request, and said, "I think we can handle this burial for you. If we need anything else from you, we'll contact you at the Mosier home."

Thomas shook the men's hands, thanked them again, and then he and Betty walked out of the office. The sun had set, and the sky was growing dim. They had been gone the entire day but would be able to make it back to the Mosier home just in time for dinner.

As Thomas started the car and they began driving down the road, he felt as though he would walk into the Mosier home a different person than when he had left it this morning. He shared this with Betty.

She smiled and said, "You are the same person, Thomas, but you now have a deeper understanding of who you are and where you came from."

She was right. He had never before felt so confident in his identity, and so connected to his family. It was a wonderful feeling.

Chapter 12

The Pratt Periodical

When the sheriff had said that news travelled fast in Pratt County, he was correct. Thomas and Betty had barely parked the car and stepped towards the Mosier porch before Florence ran out of the house to meet them. She started talking quickly about the story she heard from her schoolfriends about a body found in a cave by the creek. May Mosier came outside the meet them as well, with a concerned look on her face and a reprimand for Florence. Betty and Thomas felt so exhausted and had spent the car ride deciding how to tell May and Lester all that had transpired. They were a bit relieved that the Mosiers seemed to have already heard the news about Creek Road.

Sharing all that had happened, including what had occurred at the sheriff's office, was easier than they thought. May had urged them to come inside and sat them down at the kitchen table with hot tea and a dinner of stew and boiled potatoes. The food and drink restored them, and Thomas began telling the Mosiers about the day, from the gravesite visit to the newspaper photograph. Once he began speaking, he found that he was eager to tell the entire story. It was cathartic, like a heavy weight was being lifted from his chest. The truth about his parents, especially about his father, had been buried for far too long. It was gratifying to give a voice to what had happened to Phillip Sebastian, and to lay the rumors of his disappearance to rest.

May and Lester were astonished to hear what had happened, and amazed that Thomas and Betty made so many discoveries. When they told May about locating May Bell Sebastian's headstone, and the emblem of the Order of the Eastern Star etched upon it, she exclaimed happily that she was also a member of the organization. She offered to answer any questions they may have about it. It was wonderful to learn this about May Bell, she said, because it offered a glimpse into who she was. Thomas and Betty thoroughly agreed. It was important for Thomas to know that his mother was not only a poet, but also a woman who had strong ties to the community.

The Mosiers were equally in awe to hear about the Pratt Café, and to see the framed photograph of Thomas as a baby in his parents' arms. It made his parents feel real, more so than the other photographs of May Bell did. In addition, he was thrilled to see his father as a young man and a proud, new parent. Betty enjoyed looking at the photograph as well. She immediately detected that Thomas had inherited his father's features. Phillip Sebastian and Thomas shared the same facial structure and lean build. They also shared the same smile. The photograph was a traditional family portrait, and in the style of those portraits, May Bell and Phillip wore serious expressions. However, there was a slight lift to the corners of Phillip's mouth. It reminded Betty of the times she had seen Thomas start to smile. It made her think that, at the moment the photograph was taken, Phillip Sebastian was happy with his marriage and his growing family. The photographer had captured a beautiful moment.

Betty hoped that Thomas would always think about his father as he was in that photograph. The shock of finding Phillip's remains in the cave was still fresh, and Betty had not fully processed it yet. Thomas had not processed it either, and was too absorbed with everything else that had happened. For now, he was satisfied about learning the truth, and seeing the story in tomorrow's newspaper. It made him feel empowered, and it was that feeling which gave him continued strength to talk about his parents and the carriage accident.

The evening quickly grew late as they talked together. May and Lester were certain that Sarah, May's mother, would be eager to hear all of this news. Thomas and Betty would be heading to Oklahoma the day after the next to see Sarah. In the meantime, they planned to stay at the Mosier house to see Florence off to school while May and Lester went to work.

By ten-o-clock, May and Lester bid them a goodnight and headed upstairs to retire. Florence had already gone to bed hours ago. Betty and Thomas promised to come down early in the morning to have breakfast with them. They were tired, but the excitement of the day lingered with them, so they stayed downstairs in the kitchen for a little while longer. They sipped hot tea and continued to chat.

"I am truly a Sebastian," Thomas said, with a hint of awe and pride in his voice.

Betty smiled and felt happy to see him so satisfied. "Who would have thought that a bookmark tucked in the pages of a manuscript would lead us here?" she responded, with a sigh. She referred to Thomas' bookmark, which she had found last year, hidden between the pages of the manuscript Thomas was editing. The bookmark had the lines of a poem by May Bell Sebastian written on it. At that time, May Bell Sebastian was just Betty's favorite poet. She had not known that she was also Thomas' deceased mother. Everything they had learned had stemmed from that bookmark. All three of them had a connection to literature, writing, and books—May as the poet, Betty as the bookshop owner, and Thomas as the publisher and editor. It was particularly fitting, Betty thought, that this journey had started with a poem on a bookmark and would end with a story in a newspaper.

Thomas looked at her fondly, entwining her hand in his, and said softly, "Our journey is not yet over. We're just getting to the next chapter."

As they ascended the stairs at half past ten, Thomas quietly said, "I'd like to make it publicly known that my name is Sebastian." He did not expand on this, but Betty could tell that he had a plan in mind. He then said, "I want Violet to know, and I want her to hear it from *me*."

Betty could hear the note of satisfaction in voice. She remembered what Violet had said in the letter to Thomas: *You are an Erwinshire. You were never a Sebastian, and you never will be.* The thought of telling Violet that Thomas was, unequivocally, a Sebastian was immensely satisfying. Betty, too, wanted Violet to know, and she was interested to hear Thomas' plan on making his name public.

He bid her goodnight, and they both retired to their rooms feeling enthusiastic about what would happen next as they prepared to go to Oklahoma.

Unlike the previous evening, sleep came quickly and easily. It was deep and dreamless, and they felt well-rested when they awoke in the morning.

ଔ

The Pratt Periodical, fresh from the press, lay on the kitchen table along with a jar of milk that had been delivered that morning. When Betty and Thomas came downstairs, the Mosier family was there in the kitchen. May was brewing coffee, and Lester was seated at the table eating a piece of toast and reading the paper. Florence was by the sink, waiting for her mother to give her a glass for her milk.

"Top of the morning," Lester greeted cheerfully. He gestured towards the paper. "You've made the front page, Thomas."

Betty and Thomas eagerly took a seat at the table to look at paper. On the front page, the headline read,

"23-YEAR-OLD CASE FINALLY SOLVED!"

Underneath the headline was the photograph of Thomas that had been taken at the sheriff's office. He stood next to the sheriff, holding up his father's pocket watch. The caption below the photo read, "Thomas Sebastian, instrumental in solving mystery of father Phillip Sebastian's death. Thomas with Pratt County Sheriff, holding pocket watch found with Phillip Sebastian's body." The story went on to read,

On the evening of May 31, 1897, a carriage transporting Pratt, Kansas residents Phillip and May Sebastian overturned and rolled down a ravine at the area now known

as Creek Road. The carriage was destroyed and the accident left no survivors. Authorities located and identified all victims except for Phillip Sebastian.

Presumed dead, but unable to locate the body, the case has remained open and unsolved for years…until the day a man walked into Pratt County Sheriff's Office stating he was Phillip Sebastian's son.

Yesterday, March 10, 1921, children playing near the creek and caves at Creek Road stumbled across the body of a person long-deceased. The sheriff's office and coroner did an investigation and initial reports suggest the remains are over twenty-years old (More Information to come from Sheriff's Office later this week). Thomas Sebastian, pictured above, came into the sheriff's office at around one-o-clock in the afternoon. He stated his name, and said he had come to inquire about a twenty-year old carriage accident involving his father, Phillip Sebastian. In a startling unfolding of events, the body in the cave was confirmed to be Phillip Sebastian, Thomas Sebastian's identity was confirmed, and a case long presumed to be unsolvable was solved.

Now, who is Thomas Sebastian, and how did he come to be in Pratt County, Kansas?

Read on to learn more…

The story continued on the next page, and described Thomas' background, his knowledge of the carriage accident, and his journey to find out more information about his deceased parents. This all came from the information Thomas had provided at the sheriff's office.

It made quite a story and was sure to be the talk of the town that day. Betty and Thomas were quiet as they bent over the paper to read. When they were finished, Thomas looked up at May and Lester and said, "Is there a way I can get an extra copy of this?"

"Yes, of course," May replied, and poured him a cup of coffee. "Lester will pick up extra papers at the drug store." Lester nodded in response. "And, if you venture into town today," May continued with a small smile, "Folks will likely just hand you a paper. Be prepared, though, to be the center of attention and answer a lot of questions."

Thomas laughed. "I think Betty and I will stay here for the day."

"I thought so," May responded brightly. "You must be tired after yesterday. Feel free to relax on the porch. Lester and I will be gone most of the day, but Florence gets home from school at two-o-clock."

"That's perfect, thank you," Betty replied. "We'd be happy to make sure Florence gets to school all right, and we'll be here when she comes home."

May smiled gratefully and looked over at her daughter. "What do you think, Florence? Can you be a good hostess for Betty and Thomas?"

Florence, who was eating a plate of toast and eggs, wiped her mouth with her napkin and nodded. "Yes, Mama," she said. "I'll show them the dogs and horses."

May looked at Florence with an amused expression. Betty and Thomas presumed that having Florence show them dogs and horses was not quite what May had in mind. Still, they were happy to stay at the house for the day and spend time with Florence in the afternoon. They told Florence that they were excited to see the animals. This put her in a good mood for the remainder of breakfast.

Soon, May and Lester left the house to go to work. Lester went on his way to the drug store, while May went to the local hospital where she worked as a nurse. At eight-o-clock, Betty and Thomas watched Florence walk to the schoolhouse just down the road. She waved them goodbye enthusiastically, and they could tell that she was eager to come back in the afternoon.

೮೩

The house was cool and quiet after all of the Mosiers left. Thomas and Betty stood standing on the porch for a little while after Florence had waved to them, enjoying the breeze. Thomas uttered a soft sigh as he gazed out across the landscape. Betty turned to look at him and noticed a slight tiredness in his eyes. He caught her glance and smiled softly.

"It's nice to be able to relax a bit today, isn't it?" she said.

"Yes," he replied, and drew a hand over his eyes before taking a seat in a rocking chair. "I slept well last night but am feeling a little tired just now." He shrugged. "Perhaps it's all the excitement from yesterday."

Betty looked at him kindly. "Why don't you go up and rest?" she suggested. "I'm fine. I have some writing to do, and this is a perfect day for it."

Thomas looked hesitant for a moment, and Betty assured him that she would knock on his door before Florence returned home. He gave in then and said he would go upstairs to rest for just a while and come down again for lunch.

Betty nodded and watched him walk back into the house. She was glad he was taking some time to rest. After the busy pace they had kept, she was sure he needed it. She entered the house shortly afterwards to fetch her journal from her room. She did, in fact, have some writing to do. After they had returned home last night and talked to the Mosiers, she had been too tired to write in her journal. Now, with the house quiet and Thomas resting, it was an ideal time for her to update her journal with yesterday's events.

She spent the remainder of the morning doing just that. As she came to the description of Thomas having his photograph taken for the paper, she thought that it would be nice to paste a clipping from the paper on her page. She was glad that Thomas had asked about getting extra copies. Apart from memorializing the moment in her journal, Betty knew that her friends and family back in Oregon would love a copy. The Highleys, and Bea, especially, would be excited to read the story and to see Thomas' photo on the front page.

There was another person who should see the paper too, she thought. That person was Thomas' aunt, Violet. Perhaps the newspaper would be Thomas' way of letting her know that he had assumed the surname Sebastian. She planned to revisit this with him later. For now, she would let him rest.

She retired to the porch and imagined what she would say to her mother and friends when they returned to Marshfield.

Coos County, Oregon already felt like a foreign place after experiencing the train ride and Pratt, Kansas. Thomas had said to her yesterday, on the drive back, that he felt like a different person. Betty realized that she also felt different and wondered what effect that would have once they returned to their routines in Marshfield. It was an odd feeling to think about returning, as so much had been revealed in the short time they had been in Kansas.

What else could happen, and what else would reveal itself over the remainder of the trip, she wondered. She sat back in the rocking chair and pondered these thoughts.

଍

Betty returned inside at half past noon to see if Thomas was up and ready for lunch. As she opened the screen door and passed the kitchen, she could see Thomas already by the kitchen table. He was setting out plates of sandwiches that May had fixed for them before she left for work.

Betty smiled as she joined him. "Did you have a good rest?" she asked.

"Yes, I think I needed it," he responded, returning her smile. He handed her a glass of water. "Were you able to finish your writing?"

"I've made a good start," she replied. "I've been documenting our trip," she explained. She used a knife to cut the sandwich on her plate in half. "It will make for good memories one day."

Thomas nodded, and took a sip from his glass. "You're quite right. Before we left Oregon, I could not have imagined that all of this would happen."

Betty tilted her head thoughtfully. "I was thinking something similar this morning, actually. We've learned so much on this trip. I think I'll feel different once we return to Marshfield; I know that I feel different now."

Thomas took a bite of his sandwich and considered her words for a moment. "I know what you mean. I feel different about life, and family, and…" he paused and looked solemn. Betty noticed a flicker in his hazel eyes and wondered what he was thinking. At length, he said, softly, "Do you ever have the feeling that we've been guided along this journey? That something, or someone, has been leading us in the right direction?"

Betty remained quiet as she thought about this and thought about everything they had accomplished since arriving in Pratt, Kansas. They certainly had been led in the right direction, from locating May Bell's headstone; to meeting a woman named Nora at The Pratt Café, who knew Phillip and May Bell Sebastian; and then arriving in the sheriff's office just as the investigation of the body in the cave was underway. It may have been good timing, or a touch of intuition, that had led them to these discoveries. However, Betty was inclined to think that it was more than that. As she met Thomas' eyes, she could see that he felt the same.

Suddenly, the screen door blew open and the breeze carried in a gold-colored leaf. The leaf fluttered gently onto the table. There was an odd lingering whisper in the air, and they could almost detect a woman's voice on the breeze.

As quickly as it had happened, the moment passed, and the house grew still once again. Betty and Thomas looked at one another. They did not say a word, but they both knew that their feeling about being guided along this journey was legitimate.

The dog was on the front porch and began barking as he entered the house. Thomas walked towards the dog, led him back outside, and closed the screen door. He returned to the kitchen, and he and Betty finished their lunch.

Betty said, "We will be in Gate, Oklahoma tomorrow, and you can speak with Sarah Mount about her friendship with your mother."

Thomas nodded. "This is so important to me. I know I can learn a lot about my mother through her."

PRATT N

March 10, 1921

Body Found After 23 Years

Thomas Sebastian holds the watch that belonged to his father Phillip Sebastian. His father's body was found today after missing for 23 years. It was a fatal accident that happened 23 years ago when his carriage slipped off the road and rolled down a steep ravine throwing him from the carriage into a small cave on the hill where his body remained for 23 years. Authorities were never able to recover the body. It was children playing on the steep hill today that found him.

Pratt Coun

March 10, 1921

Body Recovered After 23 Ye

Phillip Sebastian's body found after missing for 23 years. His son Thomas was instrumental in helping to identify the remains of his father. It was a fatal accident that happened 23 years ago when his carriage slipped off the road and rolled down a steep ravine throwing him from the carriage into a small cave on the hill where his body remained for 23 years. Authorities were never able to recover the body. It was children playing on the steep hill today that found him.

Chapter 13

Beaver County, Oklahoma

Thomas and Betty awoke very early. They quietly washed up and made their way downstairs, where May Mosier had a cup of coffee waiting for them. They had packed the night before so they could get an early start on their drive to Gate, Oklahoma. May had insisted that they take her car to visit her mother in Gate.

"I will be just fine," she replied. "Lester can drive me anywhere I need to go. I will see you in two days, and you can tell me what you learned about your mother."

May gave Thomas a copy of the Pratt Periodical, and said, "Make sure you give this to my mother. She will want to read about yesterday's discovery and see your picture in the paper."

Lester was able to get extra copies of the paper when he was in town the day before. Thomas and Betty thanked her for her generosity, and waved goodbye as they pulled out onto the road. They wanted to arrive in Gate before noontime.

☙

The duration of the drive was as expected. The terrain was flat and dry, with scattered trees and fields. They passed a few homes and other structures along the way and saw fenced-in areas where farmers kept cows and other livestock. About an hour into the drive, they also saw a fruit stand where a farmer was selling freshly picked blackberries. They parked and purchased one carton of berries to bring to Sarah Mount as a gesture of their thanks.

Just before the clock struck noon, Thomas turned down a dirt road and drove straight until he reached the spot that May had marked on Lester's map. Up ahead was the Mount house, surrounded by a few trees across the open land. Along the right side of the house was a fenced-in area for crops and produce. Betty knew, from the stories Bea had told her, that families often grew their own food in this part of Oklahoma. In this more rural environment, farming was a way of life. Cows and chickens were also kept to provide milk and eggs.

The Mount house had an area for growing corn, potatoes, wheat, and other crops. Two cows and numerous chickens were kept in an area enclosed by a fence. They could see a large windmill and a tractor to the left. At the back of the house about 100 feet away was another small building. Thomas and Betty would later learn that this building functioned as living quarters. It contained two bedrooms and an attached washroom. When Sarah's children had been young and lived at home, they slept in this building. Now, most of Sarah's children were grown and married (like May Mosier), and only two remained at home: her daughter, Marie, and her son, Joseph. Both helped out around the farm, and Joseph worked in construction with his father, William. This week, Joseph was in a neighboring county working with his father, while Marie was in Wichita, Kansas at the home of a friend. Thomas and Betty would thus have the living quarters to themselves during their brief stay.

Sarah Mitchell Mount was thrilled to see them. She stood outside by the back door as they drove up. She had tan skin, long dark hair twisted into a bun, and a warm smile that reminded Betty of Alice Highley (Sarah's sister). She showed them the back house, where they dropped off their bags before following her back to the main house and into the kitchen. She explained the layout of the house and farm and said to let her know if they needed anything else to be comfortable. She regretted that her husband and two children were away, for she would have loved Thomas and Betty to meet them. However, she was also glad that she would be able to spend undivided time with her two guests. She thanked Thomas for the berries and sat them on the kitchen counter.

Thomas had a feeling of "home" when he was at the Mosier house, and he had the same feeling when talking to Sarah Mount. She shared some of her sister's qualities, namely her motherly nature and solid stature as the person who ran the household. The house was warm and welcoming. Thomas and Betty could imagine it filled with all of Sarah's children as they came in from working on the farm and washed up (at Sarah's insistence) before sitting down for dinner. By Sarah's account, her husband, William, was a hard worker and pushed his children to work hard and be responsible. Sarah was pleased that her youngest son, Joseph, had followed in his father's footsteps. He was skilled at construction and was often out working on a project. He built many farmhouses with his father's help, and also built furniture. The Mounts were not afraid of hard labor, Sarah told them, and that helped to keep the town of Gate and neighboring cities afloat. Gate was small and close-knit, and everyone knew one another. There was not much need to go into town, as many families provided for themselves. There was a small bank and convenience store two blocks up the road, and also a café. This was a favorite spot for locals to dine for lunch or dinner (and sometimes both). Sarah asked if Betty and Thomas would like to go there for dinner, and they gladly agreed, as long as she would come along and allow them to pay. Sarah smiled and said yes.

In the meantime, they sat in the kitchen with coffee and cornbread that Sarah had baked earlier in the day, and they told Sarah about everything that had happened in Pratt. She was astonished to hear their news. By the time they had gotten to the part about their arrival at the sheriff's office, she was speechless at the revelation that Phillip Sebastian's body had been found. Thomas gave her the newspaper. As she read through the story, they could see that this was very emotional for her.

"My goodness, I just can't believe it," she murmured, as she read the headline, "23-year old case finally solved!", and stared at the photo of Thomas and the sheriff. When she looked up at Thomas, she had tears in her eyes. "My dear friend's boy, sitting right here," she whispered, and reached to softly touch his cheek, the way a mother would to her child. "And what a fine man you've grown into."

Thomas smiled, and briefly held her hand in his. "Thank you. I can't tell you how glad I am to meet you. When I received your letter and learned that you had been friends with my mother, all I could think about was coming here." He glanced at Betty with a smile, and added, "We both are so grateful for the kindness your daughter, May, has shown us."

"I am just as glad to meet you both," Sarah responded. She looked over at Betty. "Alice speaks highly of you, my dear. You are like a daughter to her."

This touched Betty's heart, and she smiled broadly. "That is so kind. Your sister is like family to me and my mother."

Betty and Thomas went on to tell her a little about Marshfield, Oregon, and their respective work. Betty shared about her role managing her bookshop, and even shared her plan to add a coffee shop. Thomas, in the same manner, talked of his plan to open a second office for his business in Marshfield. Sarah looked on with slight awe at their endeavors. Coos County was very industrialized compared to Gate, Oklahoma, and the thought of opening up a profitable storefront was amazing to her.

"People in these parts are industrious, but not in the same way," she explained. She smiled then, and a glimmer shone in her eyes. "May Bell was definitely an ambitious woman." She paused and said jokingly, "I don't suppose you want to hear about her?"

Thomas and Betty eagerly said, "Yes!", to which Sarah gave a soft laugh and began to tell them about May Bell Sebastian.

"I met your mother in around 1888. We were fairly new members of the organization called Order of the Eastern Star—you saw the emblem on May's headstone—and we were working on a charity project together. May was a leader in the group. She was soft-spoken but had such determination." She paused and smiled fondly at the memory. "I could tell she would accomplish much and would let nothing stop her.

"She devoted a lot of time to our charity work and wanted to expand that in her life. She took on a lot of little projects, like organizing an event to raise funds for the church. She was friends with everyone—just everyone. We all loved her, and she soon became one of my dearest friends. She lived in Sawyer, Kansas, about ten miles from Pratt. I was already married, with children, and one on the way, but she often came by to visit and go to church with us. In fact…," she paused, and her eyes lit up. "There was a photograph taken of me and your mother when she came to visit in 1890."

As she said this, Thomas reached into his coat pocket for his leather wallet. He opened it and took out the three photographs he had of his mother. He carried these with him always. He selected the photograph of Sarah Mount and May Bell standing next to one another and showed it to Sarah. "Is this the photograph?" he asked.

"Why, yes, it is!" she exclaimed. "I thought I had lost it."

"Your sister gave it to us," Betty explained. "She thought you had sent it to her. When she found out that May was Thomas' mother, she wanted us to have it."

Sarah smiled. "That was quite right of her." She looked at the photo with great fondness. "I remember this day. We had just returned from church services, and May was to stay for lunch. My husband took this photo. You can't tell, but I was pregnant at the time. I am actually standing with two Mays in that photo."

Thomas and Betty, who had been listening intently, looked at her inquisitively.

"I was pregnant with a girl, and I named that baby girl May. You both know her as May Mosier."

"Oh, how interesting," Betty exclaimed in wonder.

"It's a funny thing—I named my daughter 'May' partly because it runs in the family. The other reason was, I think, to honor May Bell." She looked down at the photo again, and continued, "Of course, after I had my daughter, life became that much busier. I had these children to take care of, and

May Bell was in Wichita, Kansas much of the time. She began studying to become a nurse at the hospital there—did you know that?"

Thomas looked at Sarah with wide eyes and shook his head.

"Yes," Sarah said, "She had a desire to help people, and nursing called to her. But her real passion was writing. She had a sharp mind and a good imagination. She wrote pages and pages of poetry in her spare time. It took her years, but she finally had a book of her poems published in 1896."

Betty felt excited to hear this. "Were her poems published in a magazine?"

Sarah thought for a moment, and then said, "Yes, I think they were. It's hard for a woman to be published now, and it was even more difficult at that time. But she worked at it. Like I said, she would let nothing stop her from accomplishing what she wanted."

"I used to have a copy of the magazine that published her poems," Betty shared. "My father showed it to me when I was young, and the first time I read her poems…" she paused and closed her eyes for a moment. "I fell in love with her writing. She is my favorite poet."

Thomas looked over at Betty and smiled. "That's how this entire journey started, actually," he said to Sarah. "Betty shared that with me, and I told her that May Bell was my mother. From that point on, we were on a journey to find the truth about what happened to her." He placed his hand on top of Betty's on the table. "And that is what led us here."

Sarah looked at them with a glint in her eye and a smile, and then sighed as if in response to a memory. "May Bell had a way of connecting people, and bringing people together," she said. "That is what made her so effective in the Order, and so well-liked. She had a good heart, and people were attracted to that."

Thomas nodded, eager to take in every bit of information he could.

"Your father was attracted to that," Sarah continued, and then paused to take a sip of coffee. "I met him once, when they came by to visit. They had just started seeing one another, and May wanted to introduce him to me. I could tell, right away, that they were taken with each other. Phillip looked at May like he had never seen anyone quite so beautiful. May wasn't looking to be married, but she completely fell in love with Phillip. I could see it in her eyes. He was a teacher at a high school in Wichita, and she met him by chance when they shared a train ride from Wichita to Topeka. May was on her way to a small hospital for some of her nursing classes, and Phillip was going to a teacher's conference.[12] This would have been in the winter of 1894. Soon after that is when they came here to visit, and they got married in 1895."

She paused and looked at Thomas. "They had you in 1896. I'm sure that photo you have was taken not long after you were born." Thomas had shown her the photograph that Nora at the Pratt Café had given to him.

---

[12] High schools in the 1890s were organized under a State Teacher's Association, which held an annual meeting. At these meetings, the State Superintendent would be present and topics of discussion would include: curriculum development, class organization, and athletics in schools. Phillip Sebastian, as a Kansas teacher, likely would have attended a conference like the one held in 1895 in Topeka. For more information, see the January 10, 1895 edition of the *Journal of Education*, with an excerpt on Kansas Teachers.

He nodded, and then asked, "Did you go to their wedding?"

"No," she responded, shaking her head. "I can't remember why, but likely one of the girls was sick. May wrote to me about it and said it would be a small affair at a church in Wichita. I didn't see much of her after that. The last time was in 1896, shortly after she had you. I made the visit to her home in Kansas that time. She was just over the moon about you."

Thomas drew in a shaky breath as he listened.

"That year, she was truly happy," Sarah continued softly. "She was getting her poems out in print and becoming a successful writer. She had a husband who was good to her, and she was a new mother." She looked up at Thomas and her eyes grew misty. "She loved you, Thomas," she whispered.

Thomas rested his head in his hands for a moment. To hear about his mother's life, her passions, and her friendship with Sarah, meant everything to him. She had been happy to be a mother. She had been happy to be *his* mother. Hearing that she loved him made him feel as though his heart were being blanketed in warmth. The space in his heart that had been empty for so long was finally being filled.

Sarah gently placed her hand on his. "When I visited her, she brought me right over to your cradle and said, 'This is my son, Thomas Ernest Sebastian.' She was very proud."

Thomas breathed in deeply. For a few moments, they were all silent, taking time to remember this woman who had brought all of them together.

"Thank you," Thomas murmured.

"You're welcome," Sarah replied. "You deserve to know all of this. They are your family." Sarah said these words as if it was a matter of importance that Thomas know about his parents. There was no reason why his parents' stories should be kept hidden.

"Did my mother ever talk about her sister, Violet?" he asked.

"No," Sarah responded. "I knew that she had a sister but May never talked about her."

Thomas glanced at Betty, who was not surprised to hear this. She knew, from the letter Violet wrote to Thomas, that Violet had harbored some jealousy against May. There may have been tension between the sisters for many years.

"I remember you saying that Violet raised you," Sarah continued.

"Yes," Thomas answered. "But Violet never spoke about my mother, and I sometimes had the impression that she believed *she* was my mother."

Betty bit her lip. Thomas' impression was correct.

"I don't know if they got along well," Sarah offered, with a shake of her head. "And it pains me to hear that it's taken so long for you to learn about May and Phillip."

Thomas closed his eyes briefly and shook his head, as if to clear the cobwebs of his distressed relationship with Violet. "I'm just grateful to know everything now," he said, "And to reclaim my birthname. For years, I've gone by the name Erwinshire, but that's not who I truly am."

"As your mother said, you are Thomas Ernest Sebastian," Sarah replied, and Thomas straightened in his chair. "You are a Sebastian through and through, from what I can see, and that is something to be proud of. I would attest to that against anyone who asks."

Thomas responded with gratitude, "I appreciate that very much, Mrs. Mount. And I do want it to be formally known that my name is Sebastian."

Sarah looked at him in a curious and thoughtful way. "There may be a way to accomplish that. It takes some paperwork and a visit to the courthouse, but it will certainly declare you a Sebastian."

Betty and Thomas stared at Sarah, eager to know her idea.

Chapter 14

Pratt County Courthouse

"Come," Sarah said, standing up and glancing at the clock on the wall. "Let's go to the café down the road for an early supper. We can continue our talk there."

While they wished to hear Sarah's idea right away, they agreed. The time had flown. It was already half past four, and it would be nice to have a leisurely supper. After freshening up, they drove the short distance to the café. It was similar to the Pratt Café. Everyone knew Sarah and were eager to meet her two guests. The moment Sarah introduced Thomas by his full name, he was immediately remembered as May Bell's son. The owner of the café, who had known May Bell personally, shook Thomas' hand firmly, and said, "It's good to see you back home, Mr. Sebastian." They sat at a table and were brought iced tea. The café insisted that the meal was on them.

As they sat, Betty leaned close to Thomas to whisper, "You are quite well-known now. I suppose we can't pay for Sarah's meal."

Thomas responded with a slight smile but knew that they certainly would not be able to pay now. It was a bit overwhelming for Thomas to receive so much attention, and even more incredible that so many in Kansas and Oklahoma knew and remembered his mother. It was a new and wonderful experience. After Thomas had finished saying hello to all those who remembered him, they settled in at their table.

"All right," Sarah said, taking a sip of her iced tea. "Now we can talk. I hope that wasn't too surprising for you," she added, with a glance at Thomas.

He smiled. "No, it's all right. I'm just amazed at how many people knew, and remembered, my mother."

Sarah merely smiled. "Thomas, you said that you want to formally make your name known. You can do that through a delayed birth certificate."

Realization dawned across his face, and across Betty's. A delayed birth certificate would certainly achieve his goal. He had never been issued one at birth, as far as he knew. When Aunt Violet had taken him in, and more or less adopted him into the Erwinshire family, it had been very informal. For children born in the southern and midwestern states, this was not uncommon. Many families documented births by writing an infant's name and birth date in a Bible. Otherwise, some births were not recorded at all. Thomas had been born in Kansas in 1896, and he doubted if any records of his birth existed.

Sarah confirmed his thoughts. "Almost no one was issued a birth certificate in those days," she explained. "Even now, it's one of those formalities that are not often followed." She gave them an amused smile. "I have served as a witness for a good number of people now who sought a delayed birth certificate."

"Really?" Betty responded with interest.

Sarah nodded emphatically. "Many babies are born at home, and the birth is not recorded. It is years later that they might need a birth certificate. I would be glad to ride up to Pratt with you tomorrow and we can go to the courthouse. A judge will take statements from you and I to confirm your identity, and then the certificate is printed right away."

Thomas' eyes brightened at this suggestion.

"I would enjoy seeing my daughter May, and my granddaughter Florence, while we're in Pratt," Sarah continued. "I can let my neighbors know and leave a note for my husband. That will be just fine. "

"Thank you," Thomas replied, conveying in those words all of the appreciation he had. "That sounds wonderful. This means so much to me."

"I know it does," Sarah responded with a kind smile. "I am also doing this for your parents. They would want you to be known as Thomas Sebastian."

The three of them spent the remainder of supper planning for the following day. Betty and Thomas' original plan to stay in Oklahoma for two days changed slightly. They would stay the night at the Mount house, and then all three would drive back to Pratt, Kansas in the morning. From there, they would go to Pratt County Courthouse to obtain Thomas' delayed birth certificate. Afterwards, they would return to the Mosier house so that Sarah could spend time with her daughter, son-in-law, and granddaughter. Betty and Thomas would remain, they decided, because they were leaving to return to Marshfield, Oregon the following day. It would be easier to get to the train station in Wichita from Pratt. This had been a fast trip, and they could not believe that they would be on the return train so soon. They wished to make the most of their remaining time with the Mounts and Mosiers, who truly felt like family to them now.

Once they were back at the Mount house after supper, Sarah went into the kitchen to make sandwiches for the next day's drive. This allowed Betty and Thomas some time to explore the grounds and chat.

It had been quite a journey, filled with revelations. Betty was ecstatic for Thomas. He had received much information about his parents and would be declaring his relationship to them through the delayed birth certificate. This is what

Thomas had always wanted, and Betty hoped that he was happy.

By the look in his eyes, which shined brightly in a way she had not seen before, she knew that he was.

ℭℨ

The following day started early, with Sarah, Betty, and Thomas leaving at seven in the morning to drive back to Pratt. The day moved along at a hectic pace as soon as they arrived at the Mosier house. From that point on, they stayed busy accomplishing everything they had set out to do. The Mosiers were not at home when they arrived, so Betty and Thomas merely dropped off their bags and said a quick "hello" to the dog. Then, they headed into town.

Pratty County Courthouse was a large and stately building, constructed from red brick with a solid, stone foundation. A set of stone steps led up to the front entrance, which featured colonial-style columns. The building had four corner towers and a pyramidal tile roof. On top of the main roof was a statue of "Lady Justice."[13] This grand architecture made the day even more momentous for Thomas. As he walked up the stone steps, he realized just how important this occasion was.

Sarah's explanation of the proceedings to obtain a delayed birth certificate were just as she had described. Thomas stated his name, and Sarah attested to his identity on the Bible. The Judge granted their request instantly, and within

---

[13] The Pratt County Courthouse was built in 1910 by architect George P. Washburn, who designed a total of thirteen courthouses in Kansas. Washburn's designs were notable for the brick exteriors, four square corner towers, and pyramidal roofs.

the hour Thomas walked out of the courthouse with copies of his freshly printed birth certificate. The pride on his face was apparent. Holding the certificate in his hands made him feel whole and complete. The certificate bore his signature, and Sarah's signature as a witness. It clearly listed May Bell and Phillip as his parents, and his full name. This offered concrete evidence of his birth and parentage, and his ties to Pratt County.

It was now undisputable that he was a Sebastian. Violet Erwinshire could not deny that, and neither could anyone else, Thomas thought, as he drove with Sarah and Betty back to the Mosier house. He looked forward to sending the Pratt Periodical along with a copy of his birth certificate to Violet. He felt that she deserved to see it.

ଔ

The afternoon and early evening were spent updating the Mosiers. May was thrilled to see her mother, Sarah, and to hear about their successful trip to the courthouse. Florence was excited to see her grandmother as well. Sarah had a soft spot for all of her grandchildren and often spoiled them with gifts and attention. Florence was no exception. Sarah gave Florence the berry tart that she had brought with her and urged May to allow Florence extra time to play outside. May, who usually called her daughter inside before the sun set, allowed her to stay out on this occasion. Everyone was in high spirits, and it was a very enjoyable evening. They all gathered in the kitchen, sitting at the table with heaping portions of the soup, potatoes, and vegetables May had prepared, and talked for hours. Thomas and Betty cherished this time with them. It would be coming to an end soon, and they did not know when they would see them again.

Just as the evening was winding to a close, they received a surprise visitor. Florence, who was sitting on the porch with the dog, noticed a car coming up the road, and called to her mother. May stepped outside to investigate, and then called to Sarah with pleasure in her voice. "Mother, you'd better come out and see who is here."

Sarah went outside to join May and Florence. Betty and Thomas could hear her exclaim, "Well, I'll be darn!" Intrigued, they came out onto the porch as well, followed by Lester.

Two men stepped out of the car, one older and one younger. They both wore tall hats and working clothes, and the younger of the two looked to be around sixteen years old. The older man walked up to Sarah, lowered his hat, and kissed her on the cheek. Betty and Thomas realized then that he must be Sarah's husband, and guessed that the younger man was her son.

"What in the world are you two doing here?" Sarah said fondly. "I thought you were working near home."

"We got a call to do some construction in Wichita this morning, and were just driving back home," the older man said. "May's house was on the way, so we thought we'd stop by and say hello." May, who had been standing just behind Sarah, came up to give him an embrace. "We'd no idea you'd be here. Felt like visiting May too?" he smiled.

"Oh, a lot more than that. There's a great deal to tell you," Sarah responded. "Starting with an introduction." She turned and waved Thomas and Betty over. "This is Thomas Sebastian, May Bell's son," she explained to her husband. A flash of recognition came into his eyes upon hearing Thomas' name. "And this is Betty Featherwin, who is a friend and neighbor of Alice in Oregon."

She then turned to Betty and Thomas. "This is my husband, William, and my son, Joseph."

They shook hands with one another. It was indeed a most pleasant surprise to meet them and made the evening even more enjoyable. Betty and Thomas felt lucky to meet these Mount family members. They knew that Alice Highley would be happy to know that they had been able to spend time with her relatives.

Sarah was particularly pleased by her husband and son's good timing. Just before they arrived, she had been considering driving back to Gate with Lester. This would be a lengthy drive, there and back, but he was happy to do it. Now, she could drive back home with William and Joseph, and felt better that she would not be inconveniencing Lester. It worked out well for everyone.

The Mounts spent another half-hour with them before heading out to return to Gate. Sarah hugged both Thomas and Betty and made them promise to stay in touch. They certainly would and looked forward to writing to her after they returned to Oregon.

Betty returned inside after she waved the Mounts goodbye, but Thomas stayed out on the porch for a moment longer with Sarah. She heard him say, "Thank you so much, for everything. I cannot adequately state how much today meant to me."

"Thomas, you brought the truth of what happened to your father to light, and you are keeping the spirit of my dear friend, May Bell, alive," Sarah said solemnly. "That is a true gift to me, and I am glad to have helped you on your journey."

With these parting words, Sarah gave him a final embrace and left the porch to join her husband and son at the car. Thomas stood thoughtfully, his hands in his pockets, as he watched the car drive away. At that moment, Betty came to stand by his side. It was a beautiful night. The sky at dusk was pink in color, and birds chirped in the distance. It was a peaceful end to their exciting day.

She placed a soft hand on his arm. He looked over at her and instinctively took her hand and entwined their fingers. A feeling of calm settled over them, and there was no need for words. They simply took in the rural beauty of their surroundings and the wonder of what had transpired during their time here.

It would be bittersweet to say goodbye to this town, as much as they looked forward to returning home to share their story with Bea and the Highleys. They would miss the Mounts and Mosiers greatly. Betty also remembered promising her mother that they would try to visit her Featherwin relatives in Oklahoma. Now, there was simply no time for that. Perhaps they would plan another trip, she thought, to visit with the Mounts and Mosiers again and also to visit the Oklahoma Featherwins. Bea could accompany them on that trip. She smiled, and found she was already looking forward to it.

"We'll come again," Betty said to Thomas softly. He smiled, and they returned inside.

ℭℬ

It was not until later that evening that Betty and Thomas went upstairs to pack their belongings. They would be leaving on the morning train tomorrow, from the station in Wichita. The Mosiers decided that they would all drive to the station to see them off.

Thus, at nine-o-clock, when the Mosiers had retired to their rooms, Betty and Thomas went to their rooms to pack. Fortunately, they had not brought a lot with them, so collecting their belongings would not take long. They kept the doors to their rooms open so that they could continue chatting while they packed.

They talked about the day, and Thomas expressed how pleased he was with how quick and smooth the process was to obtain his birth certificate. He told Betty of his intent to send a copy to Violet, with no note or explanation attached, and Betty said that she fully supported that idea. Sending the document would signal the satisfying close of a chapter. He showed Betty the birth certificate once more before carefully placing it into his carrying case.

"Thomas Ernest Sebastian," Betty said slowly as she looked at it. "It suits you."

Thomas grinned and replied, "Yes, I would say so."

Betty smiled and then turned to place a blouse into her luggage. She reflected on the start of their journey, which originated with the luncheon at Mrs. Highley's house. Mrs. Highley had shared a memory of a story about "Thomas E. and a carriage accident," and that had been catalyst for their journey.

As Betty recalled this luncheon, and the conversation they had, a realization struck her. During that conversation, Mrs. Highley had referred to Thomas as "Thomas E." Betty and Thomas had assumed that the "E" stood for Erwinshire. But what if it stood for something else?

"Thomas," she murmured, abruptly dropping the blouse she was folding and coming to stand in Thomas' doorway.

He looked up at her and noticed her expression. "Betty, what's the matter?"

"Do you remember that lunch last year at Mrs. Highley's? That is when I first heard the story about the carriage accident."

Thomas furrowed his brows. "Yes, I remember. That is what started us on this journey."

Betty nodded. "Yes. We eventually realized that the story was about you and your parents. At the time, though, Mrs. Highley referred to you only as 'Thomas E.'"

Thomas nodded again, but still wondered why Betty had brought up the story.

"What if she was not referring to you as 'Thomas Erwinshire'," she continued, pausing and placing emphasis on "Erwinshire." "What if, instead..."

A bolt of realization flashed across his face, and he understood. "What if, instead, she was referring to me as 'Thomas Ernest'," he exclaimed, completing Betty's sentence.

She smiled and they looked at one another, coming to a mutual understanding. It was impossible to know, for sure, whether Mrs. Highley had in fact meant the "E" to stand for "Ernest". However, it all seemed to add up. Mrs. Highley had remembered the story of the carriage accident from a card Sarah had sent to her, right after it happened. In that card, Sarah had explained about the accident, the devastating deaths of May Bell and Phillip, and the boy Thomas E. who had tragically lost both of his parents. At that time, in 1896, Sarah had only known May Bell and Phillip's baby as "Thomas Ernest Sebastian." She had not known that Violet would take Thomas in and give him the name "Erwinshire."

An indescribable feeling settled over them. It was as though the world had shifted and realigned to make sense of things that did not make sense before.

Thomas felt, with such certainty, that he had been destined to go on this journey and reclaim his identity as a Sebastian.

Chapter 15

The Journey Home

The morning air of Wichita was cool and brisk as Betty and Thomas stepped onto the platform after checking their tickets at the train station ticket counter. The Mosiers had dropped them off, and they exchanged warm goodbyes. Florence had come along for the drive as well and told them to say hello to Aunt Alice and Leopold when they arrived home. They smiled and assured her they would. May and Lester wished them a good journey home, and said they looked forward to seeing them again. Betty and Thomas looked forward to the next visit, too.

They were a bit sad to leave Kansas, and a part of them longed to extend their stay. As they stood on the platform to board the train, however, they were also excited to return home to Marshfield. They would both be returning with a new perspective, they thought, and they looked forward to seeing everyone again. Betty, especially, could not wait to talk to Bea and share everything that had happened. She was also eager to see Leopold. The orange cat had never been away from her for this many days, and she had missed him. Thomas admitted that he would be glad to see the cat, also.

Filled with these pleasant thoughts of Oregon, they felt content as they boarded the train at nine-o-clock. The train departed the station at half past, and they commenced the journey back across the states towards the west coast. Betty and Thomas set their belongings in their individual compartments, and then sat together in the lounge. The porter brought them cups of coffee. They listened to the soft music that hummed from a Victrola and gazed out the window watching the terrain. It had been an eventful trip thus far, and they looked forward to some respite. They would spend the day leisurely, talking about the fond memories they had made in Kansas and Oklahoma. The luxurious accommodations of the train—comfortable sleeping cars, beautifully designed dining areas, and grand lounges—provided the perfect atmosphere to end their journey.

ꝏ

They requested an early dinner that evening, and then retired to their compartments. Both Betty and Thomas awoke the following morning feeling well-rested and refreshed and were in high spirits when they met for breakfast. They remembered how spectacular the dining was on the train, and their expectations were again exceeded as they sat in the dining car. They were served their choice of coffee with cream and sugar or cocoa; oatmeal with milk and blackberries; scrambled eggs; and a side of toast with jam. Their booth, right next to the window on the left side of the train, was extremely comfortable. The delicious food and refreshments, the excellent service, and the gentle hum of the other passengers' conversations gave the impression that they were in a top-rate restaurant. It felt wonderfully indulgent to linger and fully enjoy their breakfast.

Betty commented, "This is such a pleasant way to conclude our trip."

"From here, it's downhill and shady all the way[14]," Thomas replied, which made Betty laugh.

---

[14] This is an old phrase meaning, increasingly easy, as in: this leg of the journey is like traveling downhill, as opposed to uphill.

Pullman Dining Car Menu[15]

---

[15] This image, part of the public domain New York Public Library Digital Collections, is a real photograph of a train menu from the early 1900s. Rare Book Division, The New York Public Library. "BREAKFAST [held by] JOINT SPECIAL COMMITTEE OF COUNCILS OF CITY OF PHILADELPHIA ON WORLD'S COLUMBIAN EXHIBITION [at] PULLMAN DINING CAR SERVICE (RR;)" *The New York Public Library Digital Collections.* 1901. http://digitalcollections.nypl.org/items/510d47db-6b37-a3d9-e040-e00a18064a99.

CƧ

The remainder of the morning, and early part of the afternoon, was spent reading and writing. They returned to their compartments for a while, where Thomas did some reading and Betty wrote in her journal. She had left off with Sarah and Thomas' visit to the courthouse and proceeded to describe the surprise visit from William and Joseph Mount. Afterwards, she dozed for a while, and at two-o-clock, Thomas knocked on the door to see if she was ready for lunch. He looked like he had received some well-deserved rest. Betty was pleased to see his smile and the glimmer in his hazel eyes as he greeted her. He offered his arm to her as they walked down to the dining car.

They began chatting leisurely, and Betty told Thomas that she had just been thinking about William and Joseph. It had been so pleasant to meet them, in addition to everyone else they had met. The Mounts and Mosiers had been very kind, and it had also been wonderful to meet the waitress, Nora, from the Pratt Café. Even the Pratt Sheriff and the other locals they had been introduced to seemed like such grounded, good-hearted people. Thomas shared Betty's feelings and agreed that they were fortunate to have crossed paths with them and to learn their stories.

"I feel as though I've learned a lot about you, too," Betty said with a smile as she sat across from Thomas in a booth.

Thomas gave a small smile, and Betty could again see a hint of Phillip Sebastian in him. "I'm glad to have shared my family's history with you," he responded, "And, you do know much about me. But I realized that I never had a chance to tell you about my college years, before I started my business with John." He paused to take a sip of his tea, and then said, "I'd like to tell you about that now."

Betty smiled and leaned back against the cushion in the booth. "I would love to hear it."

"You know I started Erwinshire Publishing with John Noble," Thomas began. "We actually met in college and became fast friends. We shared the same values, and I trusted his business sense. There was no one I would have preferred to go into business with, and I still feel that way."

Betty nodded. "It sounds like he has been a good partner, and a good friend."

"Yes. We've always worked well together—at college and at the office," he replied. "In school, we had a number of mutual friends and a group of us would spend time together after classes. I studied English and literature, and I took an art class as well. In that art class, I met a woman named Audrey Wilson, who was studying to become an art teacher. John, Audrey, and I spent a fair amount of time together in class, and we saw each other separately for lunch on a few occasions. Audrey and I found that we had some things in common, like an interest in art and history. I enjoyed her company and looked forward to our conversations. Gradually, we began to see more of each other.

"At the end of the semester, we had lunch and I thought how nice it would be to always have those kinds of conversations. I was caught up in that, and on the spur of the moment, I proposed to her. She accepted, and before I knew it, we were engaged to be married. I realized, within just a few weeks, that the engagement was a mistake, and we were not meant to be together."

He paused and looked at Betty to gauge her reaction. Her expression had not changed, and she continued to look interested in what he said.

"We were not a good fit, long term," Thomas continued. "Even though we had developed a friendship, I knew that would not support a marriage. It turned out, happily, that Audrey felt the same way. We met one last time for lunch, and I broke off the engagement. We parted as friends and went on with our lives. I never saw her or thought about her again after that.

"I never thought I would see her again, frankly. I started Erwinshire Publishing with John, and Audrey took a teaching position in Pasco. Oddly, she visited Marshfield a few weeks ago."

Betty was not surprised to hear about Thomas' history with Audrey. He had his own life in Washington before she had met him, and Betty expected that he had college relationships. She was somewhat surprised, however, to hear that Audrey had been in Marshfield. She looked at Thomas in mild curiosity and waited for him to continue.

"I'm not sure I understand why," he said. "Apparently, she had run into John in Dayton, and he told her where I was. This is what prompted her visit, I assume. She stopped by the Marshfield Inn, and I was rather taken aback at seeing her. I was just on my way to your house, actually. Do you remember the night I came for dinner, and I was running late?"

"Oh, yes," Betty responded, as she recalled the evening he referred to. "You said an unexpected visitor had stopped by to see you. Was Audrey that visitor?"

"She was," Thomas nodded. "I didn't know what to think when I saw her. She said she wanted to catch up and asked if we could have dinner. In my haste to get to your house, I agreed. When I arrived to have dinner with you and your mother, we started talking about our travel plans, and everything felt quite rushed after that."

"Did you have dinner with her?" Betty asked.

Thomas nodded. "I did. We spent it reflecting on college years. Audrey told me that she would be travelling to New York to take additional art classes before returning to teach in Pasco. I was glad for her and wished her well. She left on the train the following day and had asked if we could meet for a quick breakfast beforehand. I met her for breakfast, and it was mostly for Audrey to share about her New York travel plans. I was glad that she was doing well, and I shared that I was living and working in Marshfield. She made her own arrangements to get to the train station, and so we said goodbye and parted ways.

"I'm still not sure why she visited. Perhaps she felt like catching up after she ran into John."

Betty looked down at her hands for a moment as she thought about what Thomas had just told her. She had a fair idea of why Audrey had visited but would not say it aloud.

"Betty," Thomas said, with a certain intensity in his voice that made her immediately look back up at him. "I am sorry I did not tell you earlier. Please know that she was *never* the one I intended to spend my life with." He paused and looked at her intently. "The only person I ever cared for in that way and wanted to spend the rest of my life with...is you."

Betty felt the breath catch in her throat, and her heart fluttered in her chest. Thomas leaned forward and took her hand in his.

"Betty Featherwin," he said softly. "Would you do me the great honor of marrying me?"

Betty felt the surroundings of the train dining car spin and disappear around her. She could only see Thomas, and the depth in his hazel eyes as he looked at her. She felt his hand on hers and heard their matching heartbeats.

"Yes," she whispered. "Yes, Thomas Sebastian, I will marry you." She smiled as he pulled her to her feet, and their eyes met. For the briefest of moments, they simply gazed at each another, allowing happiness to radiate in the air between them. He then swiftly enveloped her in his arms, and they held one another close.

Together, in that moment, they felt utterly and blissfully content.

ജ

The remainder of their days on the train felt like a dream, as joyous as they were and in such beautiful surroundings. There was so much to plan, and so much to think about, that time seemed to fly by. Thomas was the happiest he had ever been. He had found his family, felt confident in who he was, and had a clear vision of his future in Marshfield with Betty. The office lease of Erwinshire Publishing in Marshfield would soon be complete, and he would focus on making it a successful enterprise for him and for Betty. Meanwhile, Betty would begin plans to start construction on the coffee shop addition to The Sapphire Key. Thomas welcomed her ideas and help for the design of his shopfront, and Betty would be eager to hear his input as the coffee shop came together. They would work on their individual businesses but would do so as a team.

Thomas entwined Betty's hand in his as they shared their plans. He brushed his thumb across the ring finger of her left hand and regretted that he did not yet have a ring to give her. He would have loved to give her his mother's ring and felt sure that May Bell Sebastian would be happy to know he was marrying the woman he loved.

Betty smiled as he said this, and replied, "I have a feeling that your mother knows, and is happy." She leaned forward and softly kissed him. "What Sarah said is true: May Bell

Sebastian had a gift of bringing people together. We would not be sitting here now, if not for her."

Thomas returned her kiss and acknowledged the truth of her words. May Bell had led them on an incredible journey. Her spirit had guided them and given them strength.

At times in the coming years, Betty and Thomas would think of May Bell as they walked along the pier or sat together in The Sapphire Key. A gold-colored leaf would float by on the breeze, or a candle would flicker with the faintest hint of a woman's voice in the distance. These moments were fast and fleeting, but Betty and Thomas felt a stronger connection to May Bell whenever they occurred, and a stronger connection to each other.

Chapter 16

Home

The train pulled into the station at North Bend in the late afternoon. The moment that Betty and Thomas stepped out onto the platform and breathed in the coastal sea air, they looked at each other and sighed, "We're home." It was cool and slightly misty as rain gathered in the clouds. Seagulls soared in the sky above, and the trees around them looked vibrantly green. They had returned to Coos Bay, and welcomed the familiar sights, smells, and sounds.

Clarence Highley had kept their train schedule and had offered to fetch them from the station when they returned. They expected him to arrive shortly to drive them to Marshfield in his Model-T. They sat down on a bench while waiting for him. Thomas offered Betty his coat and wrapped his arm around her.

In a quarter of an hour, they saw Clarence driving in, and stood happily to greet him. "It feels like ages since we've seen Clarence," Betty remarked. "Although, we really haven't been away that long. I suppose it just feels nice to be back home."

Thomas kissed her cheek and picked up her bag. "It does feel good to be back," he smiled.

"The travelers have returned," a voice exclaimed. They looked up to see Clarence walking towards them. Betty smiled brightly. "It's so nice to see you, and thank you for getting us."

"Of course," Clarence smiled at Betty, and then patted Thomas fondly on the shoulder. "Mother is eager to hear all of your news. But I thought I'd drive you straight to the Inn so you can rest. You're expected at tea at the house tomorrow, one-o-clock sharp."

Thomas laughed, "I will be there, and I look forward to sharing our news."

Clarence caught Thomas and Betty sharing a look, though dismissed it. He helped them load their bags into the car, and then started the drive to Marshfield. Along the way, he updated them on what had happened since they had left. There had not been many changes, and work at the lumbermill remained steady. Bea and Leopold had come by the Highley house for lunch several times. He had stopped in The Sapphire Key to visit the cat and found that Leopold was quite happy to have the run of the bookshop. He mentioned that Elizabeth might be spoiling him. Betty and Thomas laughed at that.

"Oh, and it seems that Leopold has made a new friend as well."

"A new friend?" Betty responded curiously.

"You'll find out soon enough," Clarence answered, and Betty was left pondering and eager to get home to see the cat.

He soon drove up to the Featherwin house and helped Betty with her bags. "You're expected at tea tomorrow, too," he said with a smile.

"I wouldn't miss it," she responded, and thanked him again for driving them.

Thomas took his bag and carrying case out of the car as well. "I'm going in to say hello to Mrs. Featherwin and Leopold," he explained. "Then I'll walk over to the Inn."

Clarence nodded, and waved goodbye. They watched him turn the car in the direction of the Highley house, and then ascended the porch steps. They looked at one another happily for a moment before Betty opened the door.

"My dearest girl, is that you?" they heard Bea exclaim. Before they could respond, Bea Featherwin was at the door, taking their bags and giving them both an embrace. In the same moment, a large mass of orange fur darted towards them. Leopold circled Betty's legs enthusiastically, purring and meowing, and then did the same to Thomas.

"As you can see, you have both been missed," Bea said with a laugh.

Betty and Thomas smiled and knelt to give the cat attention. "We missed you, too," Betty said fondly. Bea insisted that they take off their coats and rest in the parlor while she fetched them some cocoa. "I can't wait to hear your news," she said. "But I'll give you time to rest tonight. You can tell all of us everything at tea tomorrow."

"Tea at the Highleys?" Betty asked with a smile. It appeared that they had all been invited to tea. "Clarence gave us the message when he picked us up from the train station."

Bea smiled in return and headed into the kitchen to get their cups of cocoa. Once she was out of the room, Leopold hopped onto the sofa between them and purred loudly. Thomas smiled and stroked him behind the ears, and then turned to look at Betty.

"I may go speak with your mother now, if that's all right," he said.

Betty looked at him quizzically. He took her hand, and said, in a serious tone, "I'd like her blessing."

"Oh," Betty replied, touched by his sincerity.

"I'll be back," he murmured, with a slight squeeze of her hand, and stood to walk down the hall towards the kitchen.

Betty looked down at Leopold to tell him the news of her engagement to Thomas, but she somehow felt that he already knew. He looked at her with his big green eyes, and gave a vocal meow, placing his paw on her knee. "Oh, Leopold," she murmured, petting him. "Thank you. He is a good man."

Leopold meowed again, and then suddenly hopped down from the sofa.

"Where are you going?" Betty asked and started to follow him into her bedroom. When she arrived at the doorway, she gasped. Curled up on her rocking chair was a small, grey kitten. It looked to be sound asleep, but when she entered her room, it lifted its head and blinked at her with pale green eyes. The kitten jumped down from the chair and walked over to her with a cheerful meow. "Where did you come from, little one?" she asked as the kitten bumped its forehead against her hand. It was tiny, but strong and had a glint of mischief in its eyes. Betty looked at Leopold, who sat by the door with an expression on his face that Betty could only describe as "pleased."

"What will mother say when she finds out?" she asked aloud, for she had a sneaking suspicion that this young cat had come to live with her and Leopold.

CR

Betty spent some time with the cats and took a moment to freshen up in the washroom before returning to the parlor. Leopold and the little kitten followed her. Bea and Thomas were there, standing by the hearth and speaking with cheerful voices. Bea gave Thomas an embrace.

Betty smiled. Clearly, Thomas' talk with Bea had gone well.

Bea smiled at her as soon as she walked into the room and extended her hand to her. "I'm so happy for you both," she exclaimed. "Of course, I give my blessing. I could not imagine a finer son-in-law, and better husband for my daughter."

"Oh, mother," Betty responded, embracing her. "Thank you."

"There is something I want to give you," Bea continued. "I've kept it in my jewelry box." She walked over to the table and picked up a small box, and then handed it to Betty. "Open it," she requested with a broad smile.

Intrigued, Betty opened the lid to reveal a beautiful ring inside. It was silver, with a small, blue-colored stone in the center. She gasped as she recognized it. It had been her mother's engagement ring. Bea had always worn her silver wedding band, and wore it still, but she had kept the engagement ring that Henry had given her.

"Mother," Betty murmured softly.

"It's yours, if you like it."

Betty felt a tear in her eye. "I love it," she replied. "It's perfect."

She then turned to Thomas, who said warmly, "It is perfect." He gently took the ring out of the box. Drawing near to Betty, he took her hand and slipped the ring onto her finger. It fit her perfectly and was indeed beautiful. He smiled and brushed his thumb across her cheekbone in a loving gesture as they shared a soft kiss. When they looked back at Bea, they saw that she was beaming.

A high-pitched meow interrupted them, and Betty suddenly remembered the kitten. "Oh, there you are," she replied with a laugh.

"Who is this?" Thomas asked.

"That's exactly what I'm wondering," Betty responded. "Mother, did you know that this kitten was in my room?"

Bea laughed. "Yes, of course I did. His name is Henry. Not after your father," Bea clarified, as she saw Betty's surprised expression. "But the name just suits the little fellow, don't you think?

Betty and Thomas looked at one another, dumbfounded. The kitten sat at their feet, looking up at them with an endearing expression on his furry, grey face.

"Henry," Thomas called, and the kitten bounced over to him with a flourish. Thomas looked at Betty in amusement. It appeared there was yet another new family member they would need to get acquainted with.

☙

The evening at the Featherwin house was enjoyable. Thomas stayed for dinner and departed afterward to make his way to the nearby Inn. He said he would come by tomorrow so that they could walk to the Highleys' together. In many ways, it was just as if nothing in Marshfield had changed, but in other ways, everything had changed for Betty and Thomas.

Betty retired to her room later after chatting with her mother and telling her about Thomas' proposal on the train. The rest of their story could wait until the next day, but Betty knew that Bea at least wanted to hear about their engagement.

As she got ready for bed, she was the happiest she had ever been. She could not wait to see where life would lead her next, with Thomas and Leopold (and perhaps, the feline Henry) by her side.

She sighed in contentment as she unpacked some blouses from her luggage to place into her dresser drawer. Opening the drawer, she noticed that some of her clothing was rumpled. She reached inside to make room for her blouses, and her hand suddenly felt the corner of an envelope. The flap was open, and the letter had partially slipped out. Betty frowned. She knew that this was Violet's letter. She had hidden it in the drawer underneath her clothing and had securely sealed it. Who had disturbed it?

Her face flushed, and she already knew the answer. Her mother, Bea, must have seen the letter when she brought clothes into Betty's room. Bea had done laundry before Betty and Thomas left for the trip and had asked Betty where she would like the clean clothes. Betty could not remember what she had told Bea. Regardless, she knew that Bea had seen the letter.

Betty picked up the envelope and resealed it. She glanced at the face of the letter once more, seeing "Thomas Erwinshire'" written across it, and "Violet Erwinshire" in the left-hand corner. Thomas' name suddenly looked odd with "Erwinshire" next to it.

In that instant, Betty made the decision to destroy the letter. Violet's words and actions had impacted so many lives, and the letter had done all the damage it could do. It would not hold power over them any longer.

Betty wordlessly stepped into the kitchen to fetch a pair scissors. She cut the envelope, and the letter inside, into small pieces. Then, she walked into the parlor and noticed that embers still burned in the hearth. She tossed the pieces onto the hearth, where they immediately began to disintegrate. The only remnants of the letter were whispers of smoke that soon evaporated and were forgotten.

The End

Epilogue

Life in Coos County, Oregon remained busy for Betty Featherwin and Thomas Sebastian during the remainder of the year 1921, and into 1922. Thomas signed the final papers to lease out the building in Marshfield for his office, and soon began working out of that building. Clarence and Samuel, his friends from the lumbermill, crafted him an attractive shopfront sign from wood. They carved the words, "Erwinshire Publishing," followed by "Thomas Sebastian, Owner." Thomas had decided to keep the name of the business the same, to prevent the risk of losing clients. However, he redesigned his cards to list his full and proper name.

Betty signed an agreement for the contractors to begin work on the coffee shop addition right away. The work did not disrupt the bookshop, so the contractors could easily be there during the day. This helped to move the project along. The coffee shop was approximately the same size as The Reading Room, with wooden floors. Betty wanted it to be a comfortable place for her customers to sit and socialize, so she decided to place booths in the shop instead of tables. She designed the booths similar to those on the train she and Thomas had taken to Kansas. The result was beautiful. There was also a long counter with stools for customers to sit and drink coffee. The sign on the wall (which had also been crafted by Clarence and Samuel) read, "Sapphire Key Coffee." The space was just as Betty had imagined it.

Clarence and Samuel did not just help out Thomas and Betty; they were quite busy in their own lives.

Clarence had been seeing Ms. Inez Delzell for some time, and they married in late 1921. Clarence also adopted Inez's young daughter from a previous marriage.

Samuel remained happily married to Betty's best friend, Edith. They had their first child in the summer of 1921.

Elizabeth Satton continued to help Betty manage The Sapphire Key. She and James Smithson had been seeing each other regularly, though nothing was set in stone.

Thomas and Betty married in the winter of 1921, on a crisp day in early December, their favorite month. They had an intimate ceremony inside the church in Marshfield, attended by all of their close friends. Many photos of the wedding were taken, and they made sure to send some to the Mounts, the Mosiers, and to Nora at the Pratt Café. They settled comfortably into their life together, and Thomas moved into the Featherwin house. Their businesses continued to do well through 1921 and 1922, though they were prepared to encounter harsh and lean times ahead. Through it all, the blissful times and the hardships, they strengthened, supported, and loved each other.

As for the cats, Leopold and Henry: Leopold continued to make his home at the Featherwin house and The Sapphire Key. He could often be found walking between the Reading Room and Sapphire Key Coffee to greet customers or curled up on his cushion underneath the phonograph.

Henry had taken an instant liking to Thomas. He began following Thomas to his office every day, and soon became the resident "office cat" who helped Thomas greet his publishing clients.

❣

Betty had lived with her fair share of secrets. Some were small and had little impact, like the secret of her birthname, Bettunia, and the secret of her unique ability to communicate with her cat, Leopold. Others were better left concealed. Everyone harbored a secret or a story from the past.

It was not important what those secrets were, but rather how one responded to them.

Even the universe had secrets. If one listened and watched closely, those secrets would gradually be revealed in ordinary things, like a gold-colored leaf blowing in on the breeze.

Marshfield

March 30, 1921

Marshfield Couple Engage[d]

Mrs. Bea Featherwin has announced the recent engagement of her daughter Betty Featherwin to Thomas E. Sebastian. Betty is the owner of The Sapphire Key bookstore, and Thomas is the owner of Erwinshire Publishing.

Phillip, and May Bell Sebastian, and the bride-to-be is the daughter of the late Henry of Mrs. Bea Featherwin has stated, "the wedding will take place in December, as it is the couple's favorite month of

Marshfield

August 21, 1921

Publishing Company opens

Mr. Thomas E. Sebastian has opened Erwinshire Publishing in Marshfield. It is Mr. Sebastian's second location for his publishing business. The main office

is in Dayton, Washington. R[] Mr. Sebastian has spent a [lo]t of time in Marshfield, Oregon and stated, "he quickly fell in love with the area."

Dayton, W[

March 30, 1921

Weddings

Mr. Thomas E. Sebastian, longtime resident of Dayton, Washington and Betty Featherwin a longtime resident of Marshfield, Oregon have announced their recent engagement. The groom,

Mr. Sebastian owns a successful publishing company, Erwinshire Publishing and Miss Featherwin is the owner of The Sapphire Key bookstore. The couple plan to wed at the end of the year.

Marshfield

[Dec]ember 20, 1921

Coffee Shop Grand Opening

The Sapphire Key bookshop has announced the opening of its coffee shop. Owner Betty Featherwin stated, it was her father's dream to always add on a coffee

shop to the existing bookstore. Sadly, he passed away before he got the chance to do this. I am so pleased that I was able to do this for him.

Afterword

While this book is a work of fiction, and the scenes, characters, and events are a product of my imagination, the setting and historical references throughout the book are based in reality. Coos County, Oregon; Pratt, Kansas; and Gate, Oklahoma are real-life areas of the United States. Locales like the North Bend Mill & Lumber Company; the Pratt County Courthouse; and the Union Station in Wichita, Kansas did, (and do) in fact, exist. While fictionalized to some extent, historical relics, like the Pullman passenger train and Model-T cars, weave throughout this story, and are based on how they may have been truly depicted in 1921. A few of my distant family members found their way to Coos County in the 1800s and 1900s, and worked on the railroad and at the shipyard, which were booming industries during that time. Other family members lived in the midwestern states, including Kansas and Oklahoma. It was an interesting, rich, and sometimes challenging life for them. Even when they faced hardships, however, family was the constant force that carried them through. As an homage to them, and to that captivating time, I drew from these historical settings to create the world of Betty Featherwin, her friends, and her family.

Also by Sarah Jane Gross

THE TWO SECRECTS

It was 1920 in Coos County, Oregon. Heavy fog was rolling in as Betty Featherwin walked past the pier to the bookshop she inherited from her father. It was a town rich in history and captivation. Her life unfolds in the early years of this coastal area.

Fiction/Literature/ 978-1-7351955-0-6

THE THIRD SECRET

The year 1920 is coming to a close in the coastal region of Coos County, Oregon, an area rich in history and folklore. Betty Featherwin, the owner of a bookshop, weaves through life as she handles events that come her way. She balances the keeping and sharing of secrets that continue to surface. In this sequel to *The Two Secrets*, Betty's life unfolds as she learns more about herself, and others.

Fiction/Literature/ 978-1-7351955-2-0

Follow Sarah Jane Gross at Amazon.com and Gooodreads.com.

About the Author

Sarah Jane Gross is an author, lawyer, and mediator. She has spent a good portion of her life on a college campus. After graduating from high school, she lived on campus at the University of California, Davis in northern California, where she graduated with a Bachelor's in English and Expository Writing. After graduation, she stayed on to receive a teaching credential and Master's in Education and, for a while, taught middle school and high school English. She then pursued further education and attended Chapman University School of Law in southern California, where she graduated with a law degree. After passing the Bar exam, she worked for a firm practicing education law. She then decided to focus on a different area of law and was accepted to Pepperdine University School of Law in the coastal city of

Malibu, California in Los Angeles County. She lived on campus and graduated with a Master's in Law through the Straus Institute for Dispute Resolution.
Sarah has had many legal articles published, and enjoys creative writing, which has always been a passion for her.